AUREOLE

Aureole

CAROLE MASO

THE ECCO PRESS

THE ECCO PRESS
100 West Broad Street
Hopewell, New Jersey 08525

Published simultaneously in Canada by
Penguin Books Canada Ltd., Ontario
Printed in the United States of America

Library of Congress Cataloging-in-Publication Data

Maso, Carole.
    Aureole / Carole Maso.—1st ed.
        p.   cm.
    ISBN 0-88001-482-2
    I. Title
PS3563.A786A93   1996
813'.54—dc20   96-20641

Designed by Angela Foote Design

The text of this book is set in Garamond

9 8 7 6 5 4 3 2 1

FIRST EDITION

This book was written in offering to the one just out of reach—radiant, waiting.

Acknowledgments

Not without the Lannan Foundation.

Not without the muses. Not without Steve, Ilene, Amy, Bhanu, Zenka, Judith. Not without Cathy, Harry, John, Dan, Alan, Frank, the desert. Not without the desert. Not without Colette. Not without Gertrude, Virginia, Djuna. Not without Satyatjit Ray this time. Not without Indira, Lucinda, Rosa in snow, Thalia, Aishah. CD, Forest, Rosmarie, Keith. Pilar and Bob. Mom and Dad. Lorraine and Bud. Not without Madeleine, Lily, Shay, Laura, Chris, Jan, Gale and Lori. Coco and Fauve. Not without the city of Paris. Not without Pascal and Stephane. Mallarme, Baudelaire. Rimbaud. Madame Alfred Carriere and Cecile Brunner. Not without the woman with the pearl earring, Anna Kavan, Maya Deren. Not without Anne-Marie Stretter. Not without Provincetown. Not without the Film Forum, The Walter Reade, the Anthology Film Archives.

Not without the full eclipse of the moon.

Not without the Lannan (salvation) Foundation.

Never without Louis, Barbara, Laura, Dixie.

Never without Helen.

Contents

PREFACE

Who is the woman on the bridge who in different places and in different guises continually reappears? At the beginning of this project, I thought I knew; by the end I have no idea. A woman moving along the relentless trajectory of her desire, transfomed by it, again and again.

Aureole to my mind is the story of a woman who wants.

For a long time now, perhaps even twenty years, I have held in my body a single sentence. This sentence, written by Virginia Woolf and placed at the heart of her great novel *To the Lighthouse*, has haunted me. I believe I can trace to this one line my early belief that language was capable of great physical and emotional feats which had barely been tapped into. Oh that fiction, of all things, might do something other than be descriptive! Here is the sentence:

> Mr. Ramsay, stumbling along a passage one dark morning, stretched his arms out, but Mrs. Ramsay having died rather suddenly the night before, his arms, though stretched out, remained empty.

Feel how wounded this line is, how it limps with grief, how it is barely intelligible by the usual standards—as if ordinary structures

viii

could not possibly hold this level of emotion, this weight. It remains broken, filled with confusion and yearning. I do believe there might be ways in language to express the extreme, the fleeting, the fugitive states that hover at the outermost boundaries of speech.

This book was written in a blur of desire, passion presssing these pieces into shapes. Desire imposed its own excesses, demanded I abandon myself to the trance of language—its heat, its weight, its erotic slur. Line by line I have tried to slip closer to a language that might function more bodily, more physically, more passionately. I have tried to feel the sexual intoxication of the line or page or narrative, to create an open space where pleasures and arousals spread in a lateral radiance, an aureole of desire. If I felt I was doing something I already knew how to do well, the rule was to start again, to attempt to break habitual patterns of mind and expression. I've tried to write into the heart of longing, of regret, unsure once I was there how I would get back.

In this time of witness, of storytelling, I've tried to allow myself to walk into forgetfulness, dissolution. The zone of speechlessness one sometimes enters during sex, the tug of silence, the weird filling in with words that do not seem to make sense. This called up Stein for me, and her particular brand of playfulness—her baby talk, her repetitions, her songs. The small codes, love letters, she embedded in her texts.

I have wanted a little of the way lovers sound, their sputterings, their hopeless stutterings, their confessions, what is most precious to them, the specific ways they are intimate—their ability to answer questions they have not been asked. The direct plea asserting itself, the intervention of thought with sensation, the abrupt shifts in time, place, point of view, as invariably one lover will call up a past love or experience, or fantasy will intermingle with reality, disrupting the usual way of thinking. The tumult and disorientation. The enlargement of a small detail which results in the loss of the whole, the blurring of the greater picture, the strange erasures of self, and that other thing—is that you, snow ghost?—which remains.

I have started to think more and more about how these urgencies might create new formal structures. One of the greatest pleasures has been exploring the sexual energy of the sentence, the erotic surge of the phrase. Poets, of course, are quite adept at such things, but it has taken me, the prose writer, a long time to get here. I love the ability to create new logics: a logic of passion, a logic of the body dramatized by where the line breaks, or the paragraph, a logic of passion created in the caesuras, in the gaps, where unexpected tensions can produce palpable sensation. A physical gathering of linguistic forces might propel the reader to a point where, finally, all pressures are brought to bear on a single startling word or phrase.

I have tried to leave this work at its most erotic moment, longing at the threshold of story, before the shapes are made manifest, before the connections lose their mysterious, fragile hold. In the liminal space before whatever happens next will happen. Where both writer and reader are for a while endlessly possible—fluid, luminous, clairvoyant, intensely alive, close to death, reckless.

The desire all winter long was for transformation, transcendence. When I lift my dreaming head, all of a sudden spring has come, and it is Paris; I marvel as the Seine turns into the Ganges or the Hudson River, glistening, flowing through us on the white bed, on our pleasure river bed. The river being pulled through me like a miraculous, golden thread.

AUREOLE

THE WOMEN WASH LENTILS

When they are French, which they often are, especially in bed they say: *dérangement*. When they are French, and this is Paris, which it often is—so beautiful, so light-dappled, such light—the window opening up onto everything, everything: the tree-lined boulevard, the stars, the Tour Eiffel, she says, it's like a cliché, only beautiful: *croissant, vin rouge, fromage,* French poodles, polka dots. When they are French.

She says, *mon bénitier, ma chagatte, mon abricot,* into the ear of the woman until they are dizzy and mad for each other, having gone with surrender, with abandon to the place the language takes them, until they can't bear it one more minute—until—until—

When she is French, and she slowly opens the legs of the woman she also opens a book and reads:

> I picture lovers on the beach at Antibes. They are perfect in their black bathing suits, next to the blue-green water, under the hot sun. On their lips *"l'amour,"* on their lips *"Cote d'Azur."* Dark glasses, Day-Glo, Picasso. They are lost in the long syllables of desire. The elongated shape of the after-noon.

And the woman says, that's beautiful and read me more and do a little more of that too. And the French doors.

When they are French, which they often are, at least one of them, especially in bed, they say: *la mer*. They say: *dérangement*.

Ocean. Sea. Deranged sea. And they read from *The Book of Oysters* which is also known as *The Book of Dreams*: "the oyster craves salt." When they are dizzy and mad and delirious for each other, when her lip devours the pulsing oyster of the woman, they read from *The Book of Dreams*:

> To think of life is to think of oysters, all year round, almost as if you could hear all those millions of them breathing when the tide is out . . . The concentration of shore space and human effort toward the one single and singular end has a quality of dreams. *"Tout le monde fait ça ici."*

And the women dream oysters in their singing beds . . . And they make their own bed sing.

They'll notice at some point, sometimes during and sometimes after and once and awhile before, a phrase will come to them. Mysteriously, or an image in the rose light: two women washing lentils.

When a phrase comes to them, or a picture, in their delirium, their bodies mysteriously writing, inventing, making things up for this, panting, pulsing, to near this throb and bliss and gorgeousness, perfection. When they are in Paris. They are like geniuses together. They are like artists with each other. During lovemaking, or just after, they see the most incredible things. *Ouvrez le livre.* She reads:

> Every tree bears fruit here. All afternoon we eat plums, figs. "It's my birthday," she says.

I sing her the birthday song, off-key. She laughs. "You are so lovely," I say. She is eighteen.

When they are dizzy and mad for each other in the moment just before they are about to come, she stops and reads:

I suck the dark fruit of our oblivion. Something opens that cannot be closed. And I am swollen with it, and I am soaked in it. "You are so delicious," I say.

"Et toi!" We are floating. I cannot say what ripens in me.

And they are floating. They gaze out the ripe window, the passage from inside to out, and outside to in, and they dream of the fertile oyster beds in the tentative last light, and at the edge of the bed the tide pulls out. Making a sucking sound.

Oh my God, they're gorgeous, the women: washing lentils, as light comes and goes.

In the twilight. When they're French . . .

In the passage between day and night. The transition. In the uncertain hour. In the time, you who are French, speak, and I am able to attach a meaning to what you've whispered, as you approach me for the first time at the airport. And you smile and wait. *Je vous ai apporté des bonbons.*

I want you in the liminal stage. In the in between place. It means in a doorway, in a dawn. When the lights go out, but before the performance begins. In the most vulnerable, in the most tentative. In the place where one thing is about to change into another. In the hovering.

The window seat suddenly bereft of cat. Through the half light, two women washing lentils.

I want you when I am still on the airplane flying here—before I am aware of your existence; I am still dreaming you, imagining you, fantasizing this: our delirious oystering.

And you now between my legs.

Closing *The Oyster Book* which is also *The Book of Desires.* In the egg you expel in sleep. In the slur of sleep. In the egg your brain releases, yearning—in the liminal space. Legs akimbo. In the moment of—in our fertile bed.

My hand before your legs open. My hand hovering near but not on you, all desire, before I begin, *commencer,* to open you, fuck you so gently in every possible way, in every type of day and weather, and then after that—

In the moment before this forever, when I am still innocent.

Before this *dérangement.*

Before your lips which will never leave my body. Permanent, shuddered. Before you say with your lips, whisper, *mon bénitier*; I want you then.

In the liminal space. In the hanging, gorgeous strange place between poetry and prose.

Oh—

My teeth raking your fertile bed.

Thoroughly. A thoroughness.

And the women read about edible oysters.

And the women dream.

She speaks of her childhood in the country. I'd like to have you then—when we're so young we haven't become anything yet. Eating chocolate. Making a *tarte aux pommes avec ta mère.* Picking flowers.

And the women dream poppies.

Inhale—staggered—dizzied:

Your hand hovering near but not on me. Or my mouth—you can feel my breath on your beautiful, beating—and yet I have not yet taken you in. The sensation of sucking in advance.

When they're so young they haven't done anything yet. I am just a student getting off a plane from America and you—your boyfriend has just left with his famille for the sea, *en vacance.*

It's August, Paris, the streets are deserted. I see you immediately. Your beau is gone. The world bereft of boyfriend—let's call him Jacques. Little pauvre. And we meet on the hot and empty *rue Anne-Christine* in August. The *rue sans Jacques.*

They're so young they haven't become anything. And neither of them has ever been with a woman yet, I say, slowly opening her legs. And they know they're already lost. They know once they start they'll never stop.

In the moment before they are together for the first time.

In the moment before they even imagine it. But then they imagine it. It occurs to them, without too much trouble at all. They saw it in a film once or maybe a dream. Or after reading from *The Book of Oysters.*

In the liminal space, the uncertain hour, where they hover in between being one kind of person and another. They breathe deeply, savoring all.

A dream of sucking, akimbo.

They've been up there so long—for an eternity; really fucking—they can't believe it—

And they're up there for days. She looking out onto the city she has never been in—from afar—all beauty, promise, shining—she looks out as the woman—delirious—*you are beautiful,* she whispers, manages to stutter.

They've been living on fruit—apricots, figs and cheese and wine—never moving from the bed—it's a cliché, but it's delicious: *baguette, fromage, vin rouge.*

A sign at the end of the bed says: *Bar—Crêperie—Dégustation D'Huîtres.* They're all over the place—first in the bed of the sea, then a field of poppies, then, then . . . all of Paris, all of France, and dreams of you . . . oyster beds . . . tasting.

When they're really fucking, they're all over the place. (Pink, gleaming.)

She reads from *The White Book* or *The First Book of Desire:*

> Only our lovemaking could relieve the pain and longing that each had created in the other. The warm liquid our bodies gave up changed the atmosphere. It was smelly and dreamy and we floated in the world our sorrow made. We explored long into the day every curve, every contour of it.
> "Speak only in French," I told her.
> "Say nothing but with your eyes," she said.
> "Don't move or I'll stop."

They sigh.

When they're up there in the apartment, it's for an eternity and they're really making love and they're lost, and they're losing their way, and they'll never find their way back really. They're losing touch—they'll need to brush up on the language being spoken out there, where they left off . . . another life . . . lifetimes ago . . . really fucking . . .

It's French out there but with a twist.

She opens *The Book of Slang.* She reads: "Vagina may be called *le abricot*—the apricot. *Le barbu*—the bearded one. *Le bijou de famille*—the family jewel. *La bonbonnière. La chagatte.*"

And she reads from *The White Book* which is sometimes called *The Fourth Book of Desire:*

> In the morning an old woman brings deux café crèmes, deux croissants.
> She comes in quickly, slows up and smiles. She has seen stranger things than two naked women in a small bed together. The room smells familiar. There's a warm breeze.
> "I want you."
> Each word a boat.
> "I want you to examine." And we begin again the elaborate seduction of sadness and language.

When they are in love with language, as they always are when they are French they explore each word, as they explore each other.

They're so young—she hasn't become a writer yet, hasn't opened yet one large artist's book, the one who has come from America, on the plane. And the other, she has not yet once stepped into the House of Chanel.

Her impossibly long legs—

And the women dream.

And they read from *The White Book* which is sometimes called *The Fourth Book of Desire:*

> I kiss her shoulder, part her lovely legs, sail across the perfect surface of skin, sweetly.
> "Please," I whisper.
> And she says, "Complacencies of the peignoir, and late coffee and oranges in a sunny chair." We make love to each lovely line.

And they're in love with language all over again.

And I'd like to do with any sentence what I'm about to do to you . . .

I'd like to do a lot more than just *italicize* desire.

Elongation of the phrase. Your long limbs in the afternoon light. Your legs akimbo.

Anne-Christine. Marie-Claire.

I'd like to do a lot more with your name than just hyphenate it.

As I set you off by commas, *ma chagatte,* that's my Javanese cat. *Ma petite crevasse. Ma boîte à ouvrage.* My little work box. Let me suck. Work you harder. *Dégustation D'Huîtres.*

Language and its weight on us. Like my hands all over your body. My little work box. It emits heat and light. It buzzes, it hums, *ma chagatte.* It purrs.

—Stop.

—No.

—I'd like to do a lot more than just hyphenate it. I'd like to swallow it. Feel my tongue on it a long time. Feel you on my tongue. Staggered. Suck the oblivion of your name.

Where language in you once again performs an amazing and unlikely feat.

I turn her over and over.

Because she is French, while she fucks she'd like to be read to. She is in love with literature, literary Javanese cat wrapped around my mouth. And I raise my head and I read into her:

> Beached on the hypnotic, lilting lip of a sweet—of a sweet, of a young nymph's clitoris, Sappho sings the world delirious . . . Haloed rosy—
> *May I say*
> *I think no girl*

that sees the sun
will ever equal you in skill.

Words dripping down and she howls.

We stagger, stutter, shudder.

We pick up *The Book of Slang* for the day we will go out. Read to me, she begs. She's insatiable. She loves my American accent in French. Really? *Oui j'adore ça.* Really? No?

Yes. Read to me. *J'adore ça.*

"Note," I read from the book, "that many of the following slang synonyms for pimp are oddly types of fish: *le hareng* (herring), *le merlan* (whiting), *le brochet* (pike), *le hareng saure* (smoked herring).

Oh, the thousand pleasures of this world—in French, in English—lustrous, glistening. Gleaming.

I'd like to do a lot more with this sentence than just . . .

Than just off set it with commas, suspend it in space on its own line and admire it. Having touched it once—escaping. Having once felt it on my tongue—but now—no longer mine . . . To have you . . . Suspended like that . . . Still.

Still. Language sends them into a delirium. They open a book. They open each other. They open another book. Listen:

"Un petit goût, s'il vous plait." Her robe falls open. Her body gives off an extraordinary light. She seems to glisten. She touches my neck again. She applies just the slightest pressure. Her touch tells me she wants more. She wants my mouth on her breast. I touch her road belly. She nods. She wants my mouth to descend to that triangle, its luxurious dark. And she too needs a small taste. She grows. She grows wild. She turns from a brown horse into a white one. I pull her magnificent mane. Press open her thighs. Ride into light. I savor the brilliant, the blinding, the gleaming—

—If you could do anything in the world what would you want to do?
—To write someday our erotic études.

—If you could be with anyone?
—I'd be with you.

—If you could live anywhere?
—Right here. In Paris.

In the half light, in the liminal space, suspended, hovering . . . On the verge . . .

In the vulnerable place where you are so beautiful and squirming, so—(pink flowers). My hand hovering. My breath on you.

—Can you feel my breath on you? Good.

Where you are so beautiful and in the state of becoming—squirming there like that begging for more or for reprieve.

Reeling. A stranding:

I read to you. My hand hovering, my hand near—but only near . . .

In the moment before I touch you: the theater darkened, the thrill of your gorgeous unknown, the thrill of the possible, dizzy. In that moment, where we gasp, the breath reversed—a place I love, a place I fear.

In the space between light and dark. In the space between day and night. In the cleft of your breasts. In the crevice, the cleavage. In the vulnerable, in the tender cleft between, in the lovely center of this sparkling . . . beauty—beauty. This utter twilight. In the place between light and dark. In the place between poetry and prose.

And I take out *The Book of Slang* in the gap *(repeindre sa grille en rouge)* between language and meaning (to repaint one's grill red), that is (to have one's period, to menstruate). In the gap between touch and speech, in the vulnerable, in the open, in the tender, in the silence which constantly changes, in the dark which constantly changes, in the tender, in the uncertain—lovely glistening center.

Changing.

You who live *dans la maison tire-bouchon.* You of the corkscrew house, that's of the lesbian world, my corkscrew.

Teaching each other slang in the place between—open your— in the twilight. Put your arms up, hold onto the bed post now and close your eyes.

On this darkened stage before everything is played out. Hovering, hanging above—in the promise—suspended in air—and the book—before you fuck me.

Once again desire has caught you off guard.

Read me more: And I climb on top of her and straddle her hips and read to her from *The Fourth Book:*

> "Women are so beautiful in their curiosity," I say, "their openness to everything. They are not like men."
>
> He turns away.
>
> It is a mistake to think that because our vocabularies are not large that we cannot hurt each other.
>
> I have gotten my hair cut so that now Lucien's and mine are the same length. He pulls my cheveux longs. "I like it when you do that I say."
>
> "What else do you like?"
>
> "Many things."

"Like what?"

"I like it when you pull my arms back, *comme ça,* like wings."

"Tell me the names of the women."

"What women?"

"The names of the women you have loved."

I look at him. He is blurry with pleasure.

Beautiful, invented one. Once again a hidden or unnoticed pattern existing in the world emerges through the magic of language and shows and shows us how to go. Read, she begs: and I straddle her mouth:

"Go through the alphabet," he says.

"Oui?"

"Commence avec *A.*"

"OK," I say. "*A* is for Annalise."

"*B*—Brett."

"*C* would have to be Cynthia. She was my first girlfriend. We were in high school."

He smiles. A universe of women.

"*D,* let's see, *D* is for Dominique."

"Dominique! Elle est francaise!"

He's losing track of the letters . . . I pull his cheveux longs. My delirious and passionate quest.

He gets up in the middle of the night to open the window. I kiss him as he gets back into bed and we start again, rotating this swollen, beautiful globe all night. *A. B. C. D.* Slowly we raise the sun into the sky.

Beloved alphabet. She closes her eyes. In the extraordinary space, the fragile space—in the place right before the heart breaks, or the line—

In the space between letters, in the shape the white makes, the fire, where the real word lives out we cannot see.

The women read from *The Book of Oysters,* which is also known as *The Book of Dreams:*

> You can't define it. Music or color of the sea are easier to describe than the taste of one of these Amoricaines, which has been lifted, turned, rebedded, taught to close its mouth while traveling, culled, sorted, kept a while in a rest home or "basin" between each change in domicile, raked, protected from its enemies and shifting sands, etc., for four or five years before it gets into your mouth.

For four or five years before it gets into your mouth.

In the space between fiction and essay . . . poetry. In the moment before you fall into irretrievable sleep, I take you, and you, again, you smiling and protesting with your eyes closed—bleary and feverish having already descended—exhausted by our love-making, language making, speechless—exhausted, beautiful, invented one . . . into dreams . . . ripening darkness. Our first night together.

It was in the airport Charles DeGaulle. She, sleeping now, held a sign with a name on it, and I agreed, yes, that is me, and we went.

—I will show you a kind of Paris . . . Paradise . . .

In the place between sleep and dream. In the movement from waking to sleep, as you fall . . . Paris . . . Paradise . . . into dream.

Into dream. Between the event and its movement into story. Between the event and its many formalizations in the mind. Before the metaphor. Between the act and the language, I love you. In the space between affection or attraction and then maybe love. Because this is France after all. *Je t'adore.* Between the language and the act—when I'm just talking you through it—what I'd like to do.

Listen to this—from *The Book of Slang:*

To have a crush on: *faire des yeux de merlan frites,* or literally, to make fried marlin eyes at one another. To make goo goo eyes.

In the space between the act and the language. My hand dripping, sticky, trying to keep up—scribbling—to get the words as close as possible, blurring hand, burning—I want you. And you put your hand just there, *comme ça,* and—a little harder, a little quicker and I find a way to say *Oh la la*—or something like that—not much, and we're rising and falling. Your breast now in my mouth, your—

And we're rising and falling. In the doorway. The passage from one room to another . . . dripping. Goo goo eyes.

It's a Saturday afternoon in Paris. August. The streets deserted. The streets quiet.

You are like a dream. All of Paris asleep. In the space where I lose, I lose—through no fault of either of us—in the unstable space and I try to call up—in the space between wakefulness and sleep, between sleep and dream—where language falters—

lentil . . . holy water . . .

God, you were—you are—on the plane away already, so beautiful, *très belle,* so hot—

Let's cool off a little—salve, you were—

holy water basin

In the precious hours—such

dérangement and—

Our delirious oystering . . . A straddling, a culling.

See them in the distance, in the place still within the reach of your eye—but barely, barely . . . The women washing lentils.

You were lovely, *dérangement.* Wildness. Disappearing.

In the body's chasms. Lost in the body's chasms. The swell of you. The shape of your loveliness. All that was beautiful, as the words fail and a particularly lovely darkness comes on . . .

You once longed for a place where language was never the seed of doubt. But not now—no more—no. The sentence barely within your reach and glistening . . . impossible to get to. The sentence hovering, suspended.

Sexy.

Sexy one. Trembling. Such *dérangement.* Hip. Ripe lip. Hover.

Hips hovering toward the breast. Your mouth at my wrist. And the way the space keeps changing:

Your Javanese cat, your *chagatte,* feeding on my mouth. Or me grooming it . . . furred . . . licking . . . *crevasse, petite crevasse.*

Between the language and the meaning.

The shape of the gap, the empty place—let it stand that way: the hips hovering . . . the breasts.

Outside the world passes. They pick up their *Book of Slang* to keep up. Paris is glisten and oyster and cherish—she'll have to take her word for it. They read from the book. Your breasts are: *les lolos* (little milk pitchers), *les amortisseurs,* those little shock absorbers. *Blagues à tabac, boîtes à lait . . .*

In the shape of the gap. In the gap between your gorgeous vulva and an apricot, or a box for bonbons.

In the shape of the gap. Hovering. Your lips but not quite. Your lips about to say—but not quite . . .

In the silence. In the moment, in the linger between this and that. Between experience: imaginative, sexual or just out there in Paris for a promenade some day, and its thousand transformations.

She picks up the book. She picks up the book: she picks up the book. The listener waiting. In the moment before words escape the lips of the reader. In anticipation. The place where anything might still be possible.

Another view in the mind, that oyster, reveals:

> He folds over the pillow and puts it under my lower back. I am raised toward him and he lowers his magnificent head to me and we meet each other half way. His long hair is draped over my swollen belly.
> "Sel de mer," he says.
> "Oui. I am salty. Soon there will be blood."
> This excites him. We imagine together the blood that is to come. I tell him a story about the ruby jewels hidden deep within the kingdom.

Your lips at my lips. Your mouth painted red. From *The Book of Slang:* To menstruate—*avoir ses cardinales, avoir ses coquelicots, avoir son drapeau-rouge, avoir ses anglais, avoir de la visite, avoire ses ours.* That is to have one's cardinals, to have one's red poppies, to have one's red flag, to have one's English, to have visitors, to have one's bears.

To receive one's cousins. To repaint one's grill red.

And she reads from *The First Book of Desire:*

> The city sparkles like a jewel in the sun. The snow is blindingly white. She is smiling. She is bathed in apricot. The poem is complete. It is true: the world is a cathedral of light.

In the moment before she gets off the plane, in the moment before she ever sees her, in the liminal space, suspended, a woman dreams: Paris.

In the moment before she'll follow her anywhere. Descend those dark steps. Go down with her.

The woman shudders imagining, in the moment before she gets off the plane and onto—

She stands at the gate holding a sign, and the sign says, *Mademoiselle Huitres,* and the one still flying, still in motion, in the airport of Charles DeGaulle, says, yes, that is who she is.

And the woman smiles and agrees *oui,* yes.

Paris is glistening, gorgeous, golden, *formidable;* you'll have to take my word for it, she says, whisking her off—we'll not be seeing much of Paris . . . Between the words and what they mean—and the one who is French is already dragging her nails gently down her arm and she is already sighing and gasping for breath. It takes one sentence.

Drageur: to cruise.

Avoir un chien pour toi: to have a crush on.

—You won't, I regret, be seeing much of Paris . . . Unless—

Already they are inside the French doors, French windows, cat, baguette—a kind of short hand. *Vin rouge, fromage,* yes.

And she is already dragging her long nails, but gently, so that the other woman can hardly feel them at all yet. She shudders in that amazing space. You won't be seeing much of Paris, *ma poule, ma petite, ma poupoule, ma biche, ma bonbonne.*

Unless we call your body Paris, my body, Paris, your mouth, Paris, your hair. Your feet are Paris, and your thighs, *mon coco, mon lapin, ma louloutte, mon poisson, mimi, chouchoute* . . . are Paris. Your legs are Paris.

In their language long-legged Paris glistens. In their language Paris throbs. Its streets are wet and hot in August. It's lit up from within and radiant. And she arches her back, and she says, ah! The Arc de Triumph! In their language games/love games/sex games: they say: Javanese cat and oyster gleam and Paris. Oh God and the Seine! The beautiful river flowing through them.

And she remembers the time before all this: on a plane, drawn to a woman or a city she has dreamt but does not know, and may never know, may never meet. Despite the urgency, the shifting, the wish . . . Bliss . . .

Having flown from the night, and now returned to the night.

In the transitional moment, in the moment—it's only a moment, between night and night,

Your body suspended in want, the mouth—the hand hovering. I feel your breath.

I can feel your breath. In the moment between night and night—in the hours in between. Its half light lapping against the darkness on each side.

Lapping and how we love each other there—on every side. In the transitional space between clothed and unclothed, unclothed and clothed. Night and night.

She taking one item at a time off me. One item at a time . . . piece by piece . . . delirious . . .

Once again desire has caught us off guard.

And the French girl with her accessories—so many *accoutrements*—there's so much to take off, slowly—in the corkscrew house, where I love you. Slowly, piece by piece—it seems we'll never get there—but that's OK.

And she's French and she's aching for it but she says: *lentement.* And *regarde: le bijou de famille.*

If they ever dress again she'd like to wear the watch called

Piaget. A *clochard, les gants.* She'd like to wear the French woman's silk stockings. Her lipstick. In our blur. In the blurring between me and you. If they ever dress again. If they ever get up again.

The Seine . . .

Lentil to lentil and washing . . .

In the place between—

Like the thrill and longing of learning another language, a second language—or a slang, delighted. In the attempt to speak—on the verge of fluency—

They slowly begin to dress each other. And with each piece another act of love is initiated. And a reading from one of the five books of desire. Until they are fully clothed—and rubbing up against each other. And ready to stage a scene in the room. The one is holding a sign that says, what? maybe, Corkscrew House, or—and the other one volunteers, how about—*Mlle. Chagatte*—maybe that. In the airport of Charles DeGaulle. But they keep passing each other—

(once again sadness has caught you off guard)

—keep just missing one another—as they might have, of course, passing each other by moments—having never known each other for even one night.

On the verge of meeting—but not. And they weep wondering what else, who else in this whole wide gorgeous world they miss. Will miss.

They are girls all of a sudden, waiting. One in Paterson. One in Paris. Waiting. And now at the edge of the bed: a field of poppies.

They shudder and open *The White Book of Desire* to make love to. To make love by.

Meanwhile outside Paris passes. They pick up their *Book of Slang* to keep up:

barbu m. (lit); the bearded one.

bénitier m. (lit); holy water basin

qui est de la maison tire-bouchon (lit); who is of the corkscrew house, or the lesbian world

lentille f. clitoris (lit); lentil

éplucheuse de lentilles f. (lit); lentil washer

voir les anges (lit); to see the angels, in other words, to have an orgasm.

In other words.

Flying on the plane, mouthing Paris, and the women of France—it's a vague, still hazy, delicious, indulgent, gorgeous, and she opens her—the perfume of it—the imagination.

Lovely, glistening center.

Opening, and the one who would show her everything, opening.

Lifting a glass of good Bordeaux to one's thirst.

Lifting her hips.

Her lips uplifted to her thirst and vice versa.

Getting the, getting the mouth around the language of her thirst she reads:

> She is standing under the great clock in Grand Central Station and she is waiting for me . . . She is dangerously happy. The day is beautiful. There has never been a more perfect time to be alive, she thinks. There is no life more perfect than her own. And she is right.

And following her from Grand Central Terminal, or is it Charles DeGaulle? And following her (in that moment—pink flowers—les fleurs) beauty, truth, liberty, desire—before either of us knows our lives, or knows each other—or know that one will ever acknowledge the other—even smile, even lift one's eyes—

Let alone—

Let alone—this:

The pink flower of your breasts, having imagined, having lifted—opening

My eyes. In the space between seeing you and having you. Between imagining and seeing you. Between seeing you and you seeing me—and you looking back.

In the spaces of longing which last a lifetime.

the women   the howl   the song

In the longing that never ends. The lust. In the spaces forever between me and you. After she, after I return to New York. Even after—

Even after—

In the ocean between night and day, word and word, between you and me. In the liminal space—between English and French, language and meaning, poetry and prose, in the suspended space between you and me. In the sexual space. In the space between (pink) your breast. In the space (pink) between your mouth (rose) (descending) and my *abricot*. A light fuzz.

The women wash lentils.

In the space between stars, in the mysterious sexual space between the howl and the music, between the dream and "I'm right here"—your beautiful skin. *Je suis là.* I'm right here.

Look—in the rosy light, do you see what I see, now on the horizon: the women washing lentils in the twilight ocean.

She picks up *The Fourth Book of Desire* which is sometimes called *The Book of Good-bye* and reads:

> He sucks on his middle finger. She watches. She has no underwear on; he knows that. He presses his finger to her beating—"Rosebud," he says.

They sigh and open *The Book of Slang:*

To swing back and forth, to be bisexual—*marcher à voile et à vapeur*—literally, to work by sail and by steam.

In our sex talk, in our language games, in our slang, in our read to me, in all the ways we found to speak, in all the ways we found to live.

Come here and I will do your parsley (gladly).

In the interstices of desire. In the space between birth and death. In the reach.

All the places we found joy. All the ways we found—despite everything—to live. The place in my brain where I imagined you, dear future, dear potential—and loved you—

In the time before we were anything we wanted to be. Oh sweet *être.* Oh lovely yet to be.

She has not yet written one erotic étude, one white book. She has not even opened her large artist's notebook.

She reads from *The First Book of Desire,* one last time. In the place of your inception, in the place of your conception, the wandering, longing for the egg, the idea becoming words, the feeling finding patterns, shapes in language wandering on to the white page—or the screen.

All the pleasure you've brought.

Between the place of your conception and the place where I put the final period. In the instant between, in the time before we are anything we want to be yet—(not even the large book)—and good-bye. In the fleeting space between birth and death. Beloved alphabet.

The child draws the letter *A*.

Between what I say to you in English and what I say to you in French. In the interval between what is said and the translation.

Between what I do to you and what I do to the sentence . . . breathing hard . . .

Ecstatic alphabet.

In the interstices. In the liminal space. My lentil and yours. So much pleasure . . . In the reach. Open your French doors.

In the lust that constantly changes, but never ends. In the ocean and the desire that never end.

In the light streaming through the French doors. The halo around your body: aureole. Between the god and the light—the interstice. Our desire. Our desire for everything: miracles, the sea . . .

> Intimations of the ages of man, some piercing intuition of the sea and all its weeds and breezes shiver you a split second from that little stimulus on your palate. You are eating the sea, that's it, only the sensation of a gulp of sea water has been wafted out of it by some sorcery, and are on the verge of remembering you don't know what, mermaids, or the sudden smell of kelp on the ebb tide, or . . .

A sucking sound as the tide pulls out.

And how now it seems, the window ledge, the world bereft of cat and music, word—the boulevard blacked out—this odd emptying (quite suddenly)—

In the uncertain moment between what you say and what I understand—it could be anything.

The shape of empty space, page. Don't be afraid, let it stand that way a moment: the hip hovering toward the desiring mouth. Or she on the airplane right before the imagination floods and transforms her—in that moment before there's anything at all—the brain at rest for a moment, perception kept at bay. For a moment—that peace. And how she tried from time to time to get that back with a bottle of good Bordeaux or a dark afternoon with a beautiful stranger.

The world emptying, blacking out, in the staggering.

In the lapse. In the passage. In the gap.

In the limbo, in the continuum, between the god and the light, the women wash lentils.

Me moving toward trying to understand you. Toward understanding you. I pick up *The Book of Slang*. In the gap between *il y a du monde au balcon* or "there are people on the balcony," and a woman with large breasts. In the gap between having one's period and repainting one's grill red. In the joyful, mysterious passage to metaphor.

In the passage between dream and word, dream and your body. In the gasp. Your body trembling, moving, alive. In the tentative beautiful uncertain. In the half light. The darkness lapping and the women. In the half light, where you will always be my *abricot*, my *bonbonniere*, my Javanese cat. In the time between a Javanese cat and I love you. If we're lucky. In the time between I love you and good-bye.

Give me your red poppies. Give me your tomatoes, your cardinals. Give me your bears. Do you have visitors? Have you received your cousins?

In our corkscrew house. Let's have a dog. We'll make fried marlin eyes at each other for a lifetime . . . I've got the fever of a horse.

Let us wash together our rosy lentils. In the dusk. In the dark. We'll live on oysters there, and sea snails. The darkness lapping at us.

In the precious moments before I have even an intimation, even an inkling that I will one day have to say good-bye.

One day soon have to say good-bye. Between the night and the night.

And the suction of the plane. And our mouths like infants, sucking in the time before.

I have seen the angels.

For the rest of her life she will contemplate this bed where flowers bloomed and urge was fed. Where poppies bled. In the gap, in the passage, in the wordless place how gorgeous: in Paris. And seen from afar, from the edge of the conscious world, the women now drifting, dreaming, reading. The women, gorging on oysters. In the twilight. The woman dissolving. In the night and glisten and holy water basin.

At the exact moment, at the precise moment where longing, where love, where desire, where ache becomes the story of two women meeting in Paris in the perfect light of the mind. In oyster light.

I have seen the angels:

Look, out there, on the horizon, washing lentils.

Her ink-stained hands

"The hand opens to the word, opens to the distance"
EDMOND JABES

Because they can't.

At the end of their day they meet at the café.

(taking excessive care—and tenderness . . .)

And he turns her hand over. And he turns her hand over
again with reverence—as if in music or in prayer.

Examining her beautiful, her ink-stained hands—the measure
of her day

Because they don't dare   (reverence)

as if in prayer

he smiles, whispers blurry holding her hands in his.

(but gently . . .)

And she stares at him in the language they cannot speak
together anymore

in the night and glisten and holy water basin

and he whispers, *don't*
and he begs, *stop*

Thinking of all the temptations:

in the garden
in the desert
in her bleary—

she wants him

He doesn't even say the word—he's not like her.

Though some evenings when he's alone he'll close his eyes:

glowing clavicle
transluscent open thighs

before his eyes.

He turns her hands with excessive tenderness. (the scars, a rose left
on her thigh)

And he gently opens her fingers. One by one. Mysterious transluscent, white. And he examines the dips—the dip between the index
and the middle finger for instance and sees

And trembling sees: the imprint of wings.

But they can't—they won't anymore. They've gone too
far—the scars . . .

Still she imagines that he takes her hands the wings of ink between
his teeth

but gently

as if in music
or in prayer.

And she whispers, *once more. We'll say it will be gentle*   gently
then

He trembles delirious he's practicing abstinence

he takes her ink-stained hands (the measure of her day) and
presses them to his forehead, as if in prayer and whispers

"Tell me one thing that you wrote down today," and she'll
say,

   "In the café they meet in before making love, he draws her a
map on a napkin."

Some nights at the café under the parasol he will ask her to read
what she wrote that day until—he can't

her hands

"They are French today," she reads, "and they say *dérangement*"

"Stop," he says. He closes his eyes (transluscent thighs) and she
looks at his hands to see the kind of day he's had and she turns his
enormous bloodstained hands and trembles, remembering . . .

It's the only way left they can love each other—

He takes her hand and she whispers, mocking him slightly and
exposes

her ruby scars

And she says to him, mocking a little, "Threads of light
will connect your palms, your feet, your side, my bleary
Jesus. My doozy of a Jesus."

the stigmata of her touch   she sucks his palm

he shudders.

He's practicing abstinence (all the bruises) they've
gone too far

She's dazzling used to it. She offers him her ink-stained hand—her bleary mystic alphabet—

Of course she goes too far.

There's nowhere else for her to go

delirious, ecstatic alphabet

She's bleary—blurting things

burning like a Carmelite

the relics of love (the scars)

She wants him wild (still, the scars . . .)

She wants him still

her legs are wrapped around him in a kind of permanent.

her want

She's seeing, hearing things now dreamy wayward martyr. How have they ended up here all of a sudden?

In a German beer garden.

She dreams his thick fingers . . .

And he turns over her hands, and he (but gently), circles her wrist and inspects her fingers for ink and says, "Tell me what it is you wrote today"

she's injured by just the thought of him

His Holy Abstinence

And she eyes his crazy halo. And she shields her face from his glare with her hand.

And she reads from her large black artist's book where she writes everything down, she reads (but gently)

'I dream that his thick fingers would know just how to touch me and that he would enter me skillfully. he is someone who is well aware of the texture and shape of muscle, the placement of bones, the flesh that surrounds them, the body's cavities. He holds the whole body of a deer in his arms, draining the blood. He knows just where to cut, just where to hold.'

And she reads to him (only a little brutally)

'Blood covers his apron. His arms to the elbow are smeared with it. He's a little shy, but so capable, so handsome . . . (only a little)'

And as she reads he lifts a hand now to the light of "apron," "capable" (just the words)

"He washes before coming to the front room of the shop, but under his nails I can see the browning blood still. He wipes his brow. He can't go on."

Her giant, melancholy Jesus. He's practicing abstinence.

take this cup

Some nights at the cafe he'll ask her to read what she wrote that day. And she'll try—she'll try to read the swirling words and cross-outs on French notebook paper. And he'll laugh and say (only a little brutally) all that ink for so little? And when she reads to him about his hair, his eyes, he'll rip the page out and tuck it under his ruby rib.

Suffering

Like a saint (her swooning Jesus)

The relics of love. Take this cup. And all that lovemaking. Written in a book

With wings.

(She wants him still.) She whispers: *glisten, holy water basin*

And she reads to him of being a little girl at the convent. And she reads of the Carmelite sister who taught her how to diagram a sentence. Her ink-stained hands. Her want.

He's come undone. He's hearing things. He sees before
him the limping, lacerated Mexican saint, her paint stained
hands and he's off somewhere in lamentation saying,

No blood.
No blood.
No blood shall be shed.

And he's weeping and looking at the bluish bruise now at her
neck. And all the wounds he's carved (the scars).

(the bleeding hearts)

They weep. This sitting at the café or wherever they are is
the only way left they can love each other.

And she asks him to take her. And she begs him to take her communion. That tiny bit of heaven . . .

He's suffering now. He puts his head to her breast, and trembles.
Her swooning Jesus. He's practicing abstinence. *Take this cup
away.* And he turns over her hands slowly like a nocturne, sadly—

They're pristine today. Perfect hands preserved, no ink, no ink, he
turns and trembles—knowing,

exactly what that means.

A bluish edge, a rage, a sadness pass before him

because he knows, because he knows too well
because he's had her . . . (brutally)

He knows she's spent the day making love. (ink—the hands pristine) because there's nothing else that's left for her—

and he looks into her face to try and see the last trace of
it—

a bluish shape

A purplish blur beneath her eyes

a nocturne   (wayward martyr)

because he's had her and he knows that all that life can ever be for
her is making love and language. They'd gone too far he
turns her hand.

And he'll ask *who, who this time,* and *who* again and she'll
sing softly to him, "must have been an angel." (a bluish
whirl)

"Must have been an angel," she'll sing whirling

and he'll remember the beating of wings.

And his enormous hands fingering her wrist and she trembles

remembering

"bad girl's knot"   take this cup

and wings and everything. Deep breath:

Beneath her eyes the shadows—she hears their sighing
wailing still unhinged detached they loved it but could not
Unmoored like that.

(the nails, the thorns)

She knows he'll come to watch tonight. Observe her with the boy
who sells a rare and ancient book. Or watch her kiss a bisexual
triathlete—in some life they would laugh at this. But crouching in
jasmine and night blooming things—

he's already weeping.

And didn't she then and desperately—wanting resurrection him
desperately

And didn't she (and desperately) dazzle

Her swooning.

He opens his hand as he watches her

remembering

must have been an angel . . .

And she opens her hand, her life to him: a blur of wings
And desperately.
And desperately then.

Make me dazzle

There is something so simple really, so lovely here: this longing
woman walking down the beach that flanks the bay in winter . . .

little seaside town
little seaside star   off season

floating

. . . recalling water: She dreams remembering the way
her eye hugged the river on the passing train—long
after the ride had ended . . .

like the lip lingers.

like the lip cleaves to the clitoris—long after,
long after.

clavicle, lilting world.

It's a long, narrow beach (blowing, salty air, sand

flying, a great expanse of gray and blue, etc., without
beginning or end), and if one's vision is good, and
hers is, one can see a long way, far. Far enough to
see what from here is only a blur, then a human figure,
then a woman—

Bending, picking up stones or shells, small collections
of something . . .

Wind blown, sea ravaged in winter she walks more
quickly now toward—

Two women approach each other on the otherwise empty beach.

She picks up the relics of a sea creature. A shell shaped like
a clavicle. The sound of bells.

The moan of the lighthouse and roses.

The relics of love. Bones bleached on a beach.

Battered by desire and the sea now she sees the other
woman nearing.

fingering moonstones

singing little sea songs

(The long boarded walkway away. This long beach in winter.
This long walk away from you now.)

Land's End—

leaving all else behind.

The professor on holiday. She doesn't have to teach
anybody anything she doesn't want—the woman on a
well-deserved break, walking, walking faster now.

Race Point.

She thought by walking she might dispel certain things.

The woman nearer—

(As you turn to go—but hesitate for a moment and
turn back slightly . . . As if changing your mind . . .)

(Now as you go you hesitate, and make an odd half turn
back. And I am startled, offered hope by the incompleteness
of the gesture.)

She bends and reaches for something.

Their bones, thousands of years from now, glowing on
this beach. Recalling pleasure, the hidden sexual
residue of their lives, pulsing.

While the woman, still collecting bits of this and that,
shells and seaweed and driftwood and small sea creatures
comes closer. Then is right there.

"You're right here."

She nods, smiles, bows her head. She sees her neck.

The motion of a hand already moving through that tangled
hair and how now looking away she sees that motion—
a kind of downward stroke in everything. The woman's
head now tipped back slightly.

her mouth slightly open.
her lips slightly chapped.
her head tipped back.

"Hello."

She closes her eyes for a moment and sees her ankles
already around the woman's neck. Back arched. Hips slung.

hips slung.
back arched.

like an acrobat
like a woman in a water ballet (the sea pulsing behind them)
like a dancer
like an ice skater

As a child she loved to go ice skating.
As a child she loved to go to the Ice Capades with her mother.

Sea whipped. Sea frenzied. Snow, now, on water. Cold.

Nods. Smiles.
"Hello."
Like the lip cleaves
Like the eye clings
ankles
downward stroke
"On a holiday."

Her knees slung over her shoulders.

Sea drunk and snow they can barely hear each other
over the moan of the lighthouse and the ocean and roses.

downward stroke.

The drag and pull of the tide.

Nets dragging on the ocean's floor. Sweeping . . .

Her teeth dragging over—

Water lapping.

The way the rose clings . . . lip . . .

As they try (unsuccessfully) to get to the end of the sentence.

Water lapping.

The moan of the night already pressing on them.

Water lapping. Night lapping.

She can already imagine them . . .

The moan of the lapping women.

Everything meets in this little seaside town off season.

She sees her ankles already crossed

like the river clings—

taste of water—

taste of—

and sticky . . .

(You brought a bucket of flowers to that tiny room by
the sea. We made love on the beach in spring.
Fucked on the pier, the Hudson glittering, the Hudson
River singing and our humming . . . Unforgotten. Bright sun.)

Taste of—

"How about a coffee or a drink?"

As bleary, delirious, the sound of bells, they make their
way to the bed at the end of the long beach and sentence,
far.

Exultation is the going
Of an inland soul to sea—
Past the Houses,
Past the Headlands,
Into deep Eternity—

She's got a lovely laugh . . . clavicle . . .

She takes her hand in winter.

The large strong hands. The muscled arm. Biceps,
tendons, the soft pillowed breasts.

"Fuck," she whispers, smiles, shudders.

"Huh? What?"

Is it the madness then, the extravagance of roses
opening in December in this place that makes them
want

"Fish Fry Friday night," a voice calls and the sound of bells.

"Huh?"

"A cup of coffee? A hot toddy or a beer or tea?" (her hips
slung) "What?"

Above their sexual static (downward stroke) and the
fury of the sea.

Her legs clasped—

Glistening and ravaged

"You're driving me, you're making me"—

The sentence hard to reach. She stutters.

hard to breathe
hard to talk.

"You're making me—crazy."

At any rate who will save us? "You're making me—

fucked up"

In the little seaside café off season they focus on
the maps and tourist brochures, trembling.

Hanging from her teeth (acrobat)   Backward and strung
up (still blurry)

Come to me.

(I am finally speaking about you—if only to myself.
It was inevitable, I suppose. I am speaking about
you. I hope not in a bad way.)

(Your capacity for wildness . . . your perversity . . . I miss you)

They study the swollen map together. Bells ringing.
"Where shall we go?" she asks.

And then, "Pearl Street."

"Or," (her hands so large and strong and—) "would like . . .
would like . . . ")

"What?" looking at the map.

She nods, "yeah."

"To fuck you on Mechanic Street. To fuck your eyes out on—

Bangs Street."

"Easy now," the professor smiles. "How about on School
Street?"

They're already shipwrecked. Sea soaked, drenched.

She takes her hand and puts it—

like a mechanic—

"Race Point," they say deliriously.

"You're making me—

Slow down a little then:

First Encounter Beach. They smile. Shhh—

Cool Down. Slower:

Two women walking opposite ways on the beach.
Two women finding themselves on the same beach in winter.
Two women, lovely, lilting, free a little, on this remote tip
two women, of land, strip of land, spit of land, imagining:
stranded.

Two women listen to the moan of the lighthouse and
ocean and roses as they approach one another—

Sandy beach.

Two women, strangers, pass each other on this wild,
windswept tip and bristle, stopped by something glinting, wayward.

At any rate, who will save them?

Two women find themselves, desire driven in waves and wind
and fierce and dazzle.

Stranded, thigh high, driving each other—

crazy

Straddled on her gorgeous mouth. Head tilted slightly
back. Or: knees over her strong shoulders. "Teach you . . . "

The tongue poised just a fraction of an inch from—

"I'll teach you . . ."

She feels her breath and oh

And dazzle.

They smile at each other, "hello." And oh and moan.
She's dizzy, frightened. She sees blur and pink and
moan and moving—sucking mouth and hollowed cheeks and
glowing bones, oblivion stranded aureole—circling and the
lapping waves of the seaside town and beach—

dizzy dazzling spit and foam and aureole and

"Hello. My name is Aurelie and pleased to meet you
and shall we now go for a drink?"

It's like a miracle then, again, sprung like this
from one another's longing and desire flung and fucked
and oh and oh and aureole and mouth and straddle

Two women in a café, having tasted, glimpsed:

A deep deranging of the sentence—disorder.

Her hair draped now on the woman's thighs. She teasingly
hanging above her trying to make words. "What—

"What do you want?"

"But you don't even know me . . . perfect stranger . . . huh?"

Two women in a café imagining

Going at each other, as their bodies draw close, approaching. Focus:

Strong, capable hands and muscled arms, perfect back and tendons, shoulders, thighs like a vise: "You are an athlete then?"

"How ever did you guess?"

Having glimpsed, having imagined:

The press of the Watermark. The pressure of her hand— one at the small of her back, the other in front, a little lower, there, just below the stomach. The press of the—

looking at the map.

"Crown and Anchor. Shankpainter."

Almond skin. Dirty blond hair in tangles. Large bones. Those hands. "You are an athlete then?"

They're fucked up, sea soaked, shipwrecked, stranded, drenched.

She laughs and says, "Land's End." Says "Far Side of the
Wind. Yeah, I'll take you there."

"Ciro, Pucci, Pepe, Napi. The Mews." Meow. Front
Street and Back. I'd like to fuck you on—

The *A* House throbbing—

—God you are hot
God you are gorgeous.

spit of land.
world's end.
dazzling night.
the moan of the fog and the cat's cries.

(The long walkway away. The long breezeway.
Where I imagine you're OK)

Up the wooden steps and through the blue door press
and hurry oh.

Pearl gray light and night approaching and the cats
stretching and scratching and asking,

With you up against, rubbing up against—

Hurry.

Sea salt and rough tongue and—

Watermark, White Horse, White Wind—

Up the wooden steps through moan and salt and swim and shudder

devouring

"You're driving me crazy."

"Good."

little seaside town off season
lilting rosy pearl in the evening light.
God, you are gorgeous.

You who guide wide ships through treacherous night, guide
me . . .

eternity.

(I am finally beginning to talk about you—if only to
myself.

You thought you were just a sex toy. I suppose I don't
understand the word "toy" in that sentence, or the word
"just."

And was it always only about sex? Or was it your
way to keep me far, dismiss me when necessary?
Diminish what we had, if it got too painful. When it got too
painful.

As you turn now. And I lose you again in the azure of a
perfect summer night on a beach.

You turn away.)

Prolong this. They build a fire. Prolong. She
closes her eyes. "God you are so gorgeous." Two women
having just met—and at the threshold of all possibility,
all-everything, imagine eternity—

imagine swollen, sticky endless night

"Triathlete"

Her flex and reach and pull and dare. Her arch and
skill and will and brave and true.

Lift and open. Ankle. Wrist and reach.

The sound of waves deranged and lapping at their
swollen sea door. She presses her mouth and throb. At
the blue of wild ocean night.

floating   humming

at the end of the world caught
caught in her pearl
caught in her pearly net

At this glistening altar. Her mouth now moments from oh

"Athletic girl."

"And I'd like to ride you . . .
I'd like to ride you like a porpoise . . .
Ride you like a saint . . .
I'd like to ride you like a mermaid . . .
I'd like to make you sing
Like a siren
Moan like a rose
Scream—
like a siren. Luring others to our ocean bed and door."

Delicious ship.

Most delicious ship.

Guide me. Make me dazzle.

Grinding

Glowing bones to stars and salt and sea, guide me.

Show me

And hip to hip and grind and straddle, ride and yeah,
good girl.

Two women scratching, begging up against each other, frantic.
Clipped or pierced perhaps and oh and oh and

"fuck."

Scream like a siren.

Fuck like a sailor. Fuck like a siren. Fuck like: two
women . . . sudden heat: you put your mouth on my clavicle

She puts her mouth—

And fast and hands, athletic girl and more and suck
and come and

Like a siren . . .

"They can hear you at Ciro's, Pepe's, Nape's, Pucci's. They
can hear you at the Pilgrim Monument,"

she smiles. Now slower this time.

(This is a message to you: not so embedded in
the text after all—I could start now right where we left off.

Talking to you even now, after all this time. Imagining,
after all this time, your half turn back—that turn that
might set us into animation again.)

Luminous, glowing oyster pearl and—

"Hey there—take it easy, Hon."

Oyster, Carmelite and scratchy urchin, clam—

Her hair now draped. She's dripping on her inner thigh
and tease and please—

"What? Come on, tell me what you want."

The moan of the fog and the cat cries.

Shhh and slow and—

rocking on her hips
rocking like a baby on her hips
rocking on a woman's hips like the ocean
rocking on the ocean's hips

"oh, yeah, honey . . . "

riding on a woman's delicious hip, guide me.

Delicious ship.

Flushed.

like women dreaming next to water.

Guide me like a Carmelite.

Sudden heat. You are flushed. A broken pier in summer.
The raging West Side Highway at our side. We are lost

in a sea of men wanting men. You pretend to want to
be them. You take me from behind. My head pulled back. My
hair wrapped around
your fist.

I wanted you the moment I saw you. Your look—that of
a deranged Carmelite nun, a fallen cheerleader, a
mischievous child.

And how you made love. Sometimes like an innocent.
Sometimes like an expert. Sometimes like a foreigner,
insisting you really didn't like girls. Like a scientist, performing
experiments.

With your homemade crucifix, your slingshot. Little
tomboy. A toy gun, a water gun you would shoot into
me. How does that feel?

Your plastics and latex and shower caps.

And I lose you again in the azure of a perfect summer
night.

Now as you turn, now as you traipse with combat boots
and negligee into that good night. Away. But turn,
for one brief second, back.

Adieu. It seems you've gone to God—or where? Though
we lived in the same city, I never saw you again.

Or though we live in the same city, I have never seen
you again. Even now, I give room, for some future
sighting, hope. Anticipatory. In love with revision,
amendments. You turn, with hesitation . . .

Our unhappy love affair. All your friends urge you
to get out, but you can't. And I, the impassive, temptress,
riveted to you. My sin: that I loved others as
well. Though nothing compared to you—that is, isn't
it, how the song goes? Your touch. Your particular
finesse. I have not forgotten.

This time they force each other, they hurt each other, a
little. Grinding hard and deep and gorgeous face and
teeth and cleave—

Triathlete!

When she's American she says "oh baby, oh honey, tell me
what you want."

When she's French she says: *dérangement*.

Sound of water lapping. Sound of—

Water logged. Sea soaked. Floating. Downward stroke. Fucked
(so beautifully) up.

In my revision, my fantasy, you whisper, you tell me you turned
back to me and fully, but that I was already gone.

And then that tentative reconciliation, unseen by me, shifted,
becoming a half turn away again where it became resolute,
turned to stone, irrevocably away and engraved and
forever.

If you would let me kiss just once those stony feet, just

once now with the mouth that—

The mouth that

Let me kiss your feet and the stone boat of your
body with the mouth that—

Two women. When they are Italian they say "ecco."

Two women. Their hair plastered to their faces.

The sound of water at their door.

Open sea. Never ending. Eternity.

When you're a sailor you say, "Hey and Hidey and Ho."

She takes her hand and puts it:

When they speak of the blue fin, the yellow tail, the
great red, the fishermen's eyes haze over seeking something far off—

glistening.

She imagines her in a fishermen's net now and she
begins

her slow, fevered
suction cupped   a little pressure   a little more pressure.

Trying to get at

madly

frenzied descent. Chewing. (a chewing sound)

"I need to taste you."

Luscious, pulsing pearl.

Little rosy pearl in the evening light.

Caught in her pearl. "God, you are fucking gorgeous."
hard to breathe.

Licking her strung up—

If she could fuck her only one way . . .

Licking her strung up through the net now. Caught in
this dreamy net and plan and trying—
tied and strung out.

"come on . . . fuck . . . you can do it."

"huh?"

"trying."

Who at any rate will save us?

Humiliated, you wanted to leave me before I left you.
But you were sex-addicted, addicted to our bodies
together and so you kept putting it off, angrily. Growing
to despise us both.

And how you made love sullenly, silently, enraged, lost
in your fury and the betrayals and sadness yet to come.

You made love desperately then.

muttering   buzzing   humming   strange words

For fun the women keep at their bedside a writing
tablet. Or else they used their sheets to scrawl—

and crawl and scratch and come

If I only had one sentence to seduce you with. To get you
back. To reach you.

One glistening sentence.

She takes her hand and puts it—

She sucks on the woman's fingers. Her ear next to
her aureole or clavicle or wondrous shell in sleep where

she hears her dreaming. On the lip, on the edge

of the known world, remembering . . .

as a little girl she used to like to go—

Summer lingering.

Like the lip cleaves and clings

Like the gull hangs in air—

You thought you were of no consequence. You thought
you were just part of a larger pattern, a dizzying
design and it made you feel sick.

You were part of a larger design. But you were never
inconsequential.

Our sad history. I loved others. I wanted others. You
could not see how you were any different. Or if you
were, then why I would not stop, change for you. Be
someone new.

Heat and light and gleam that longing beach where
they've teased each other into furious, delirious—

Make me dazzle.

There is something so simple, so lovely here, really. Where I wait
for you.

She'd like to coax the sand that's lodged here and
draw from her in long slow pulls with tongue and gum
and teeth and skill—and if they're lucky, secreted
round a grain of sand, a pearl, you gorgeous oyster girl.

sticky   "a lot of practice"

Sudden heat. A broken pier. You take me from behind.

The Hudson River glistening.

"Stand up. Don't move."

Obedient, she stands on wobbly sea legs and she fucks her
now, like this.

like this.

Then on all fours. Front Street. Back Street.

The *A* House throbbing.

She swearing like a sailor now.

Past the Houses,
Past the Headlands,

Into deep Eternity.

Far and deep.

And sleep a little.

You made love to dispel emptiness and fear. "What's that?" you'd whisper in the night frightened. And I'd check under the bed and reassuring you, you'd come down to see for yourself and fuck me there. And still you were afraid.

Past the Headlands . . .

a dream where she is being pulled with great skill and ring, with touch and look and a few trembling words—

far out to sea, where she's

stranded now. The pull of the waves and the dark—

Far . . .

When she awakes the woman athlete is holding pieces of rope and smiles, "hi, you."

And when the professor is British she says: "please."

And when the woman is American she says, "Yeah and Honey and Hey and Hold your horses, OK?"

Hold on.

"Sex junkie," she whispers.

"How do you, how do you, know how to . . . "

"Come on," she says, "you can say it."

"How do you know how—"   (tremble,   shudder)

"Huh?"

"How do you—" (frantic, gibberish, mutter)

"Hey. Come on. Take it easy, Hon. Spit it out."

"How do you know how to make such a fancy sailor's knot?"

"I'm in the navy now," she smiles.

Strong and muscled, salty, "yes, I see."

And she and agonizing slow makes

hurry

"And this is a slip knot."
"And this is a thumb knot."

"The better to—"

"What's the matter, little girl?"

"I'll show you how to make a

butterfly knot . . . " "hunter's" (something like that)

She hums a sailor's song and straps her to the mast.

Two women, their hair plastered.

On the open sea. Screaming.

She holds her hips and rides.

blood storm and sea ache—

You who guide, who harness, strap and

"pinned sheepshank"

She hums and watches, sings "you'll never get free."

From the depths of your silence and mortification and
rage you'd fuck me unconscious every time and say
absolutely nothing, except that occasional, is this
how you want it then? Is this what you want?" Stony
silence. Strangers. Violence?

"You won't be able to move trussed up like this."

Leverage, precision: Horse knot, Knot to use in a bad
storm, bad girl's knot, etc.

(a dream where months from now, the professor is
sitting at her desk grading papers and she has tied
her legs open to the desk chair with one of those
fancy sailor's knots, and now is on her knees and
sucking: the professor's hands deep in the sailor's tangled hair.)

She says, "like this?"

good girl's knot

"Uh huh."

"Like this?"

"Now you try."

(a dream in which she is floating and singing, garlanded,
lifting her lyre)

where she is supplicated
where she is anointed
where she is pampered
where she is roughed up
where she is tied securely to the mast (for leverage and
positioning)

Oh sailor girl, oh, oh—

If you were Italian, and this a movie, you'd smile only a
little sadly, and say "Ciao Bella" and shed one
pristine tear. It wouldn't be messy like this, not
inconclusive like this—if this were a movie. Not you
in my mind, forever turning and turning back—like this

Or there might be wailing and hair tearing and threats—
not this silence. Laceration, mutilations, some sort of violent
finality.

Not then to see you in every Carmelite nun type,

All over town.

I hear you are busy spreading rumors, busy erasing
my name,

All over town.

Come here, just once more, and carve into me, your rage.
Let me kiss your wooden feet that descend.

Let us go then together.

Though you have turned away now for what may be forever,
your bones for an eternity will hold our pleasure—heavy
with it, like gold. To glow, thousands of years from
now on a remote beach where we once fucked.

Your clavicle and

Beauty . . . beauty without end.

They miss the Fish Fry Friday night.
They miss the poetry reading at the Fine Arts Work Center
They miss the opening at the Art Association.

The lip cleaving to the—

The professor says, "now pull my ring." The athlete has never
seen such a thing. "Right, with your teeth. She bleats, "Ah, yes,
professor, teach me."

They're crazy for it, scream and scene and bleary—

"Sex junkie."

"No you are."

Overdosed and bleary with it. Sick. Cleaved as she is to her
now, the sailor, salt and sea and sweat.

Hallucinating on her lip:

Watching the gull hang in the salty air above us,
like safe or love while you lowered your mouth to
me on the beach whispering

last time, last time, though it never was—not for
years, not for a long time.

Like the lip clings to the clitoris, long after, long
after . . .

On that lovely breast of beach

and love and edge and sore and swollen door.

She falls into a fever dream in which she sees a woman
lying on a beach, and lifting her lyre she sings the
professor, athlete, lilting world and you and I too into
being . . .

And she writes on the paper thin sheet in desire

If I could make you shudder, come, with just one
sentence now—

The water lapping now, the sound of water lapping, loudly,
filling them, the sound, the smell of the water, the press of the
water at their blue door, only make them want each other more
and more. Seaweed. Fishnet.

Now in this position glistening (slightly raised,
one leg up) as she is about to

"You can't seem to get enough."

Slip knot. Slippery girls.

And then in your fierce, pierce, cry

Again. And then (her fist)

Rising from their sexual wreckage

She bleats "triathlete!"
Triathlon. And tribid, trible, triple, pyramidal.

(A dream in which there are three women on a bed. A
flash of three women. And the one who is the ocean,
lapping, licking—sea door—is being devoured by a second
woman who in turn is being fucked by—

and they are making a

pyramid shape. Sort of. And
they are making

lots of noises and glowing)

Your mouth on my clavicle that afternoon on the pier.

Dreaming tingling clavicle a million years from now

Recalling your mouth on the beach, bleached white

Dazzling deep eternity

the woman who is grinding on her mouth in fishnets is fucking the woman who is fucking her. Something like that—

singing demented songs   dazzling songs

devouring.

more—

DREAMING STEVEN LIGHTHOUSE KEEPER

You can't live here any longer Steven and so you go to spirals light
and even motion a circular tower surrounded by water sights
and island while on the shore you've left a modern Sodom and
Gomorrah—you like to think of it:

Dreamy lighthouse keeper mild even fevered you
hear from the peninsula of women far off: "slip knot"

and hear them whisper over water:
"bow knot"
"good girl's knot"

you're dazzled

Applauding from your lofty perch you light your lantern like a
code and wait in hope and dream your dream and wand and sleep.

Dreaming Steven lighthouse keeper.
Lonely lovely lilting Steven
holds himself and dreams of women.

In his hand a luminous swelling wand and risen

Flushed by the light of the lighthouse Steven
round and even.

white light
red light
green light

safe and harbor pulsing blood and sea and even
dreamy lighthouse keeper Steven

he hears in him the wailing of the women over water
a modern Sodom and Gomorrah the little seaside town off season

He hears a sound in him like glee or gleam

and the women raise their heads and see out past the swollen
door far off a small—a faltering beam of light

a blur

a pulsing light

a trembling

and the women in their pleasure conjure a dreamy grieving lighthouse keeper who now and then they whisper guides himself into
them

far and deep

He hears a sound like glee or gleam—wand and strum—
solitary one.

You couldn't live there anymore. You left the shore and went to
spirals light and even motion a circular tower
surrounded by ocean and sighs and safety—

island.

You are watching your happiness sail toward you now in a wooden
replica of a woman, you are watching your happiness—in the
head of a woman, a replica in wood on the bow of a boat called the
Celeste-Martine.
You repeat the name and dream.

In the shape of a woman made of wood—
in private creation—
in masturbation—

you see a figurehead through fog
you hear a sound like glee or gleam
dreaming Steven

Celeste-Martine! Celeste-Martine!

(even motion)

you say your matins
you say your matins

You're in love with the schoolmaster's daughter. You're in love with
the stationmaster's wife. The amateur astrologist, the sea captain's
widow. You're in love with the parson's half sister—
a bonnie crew, a pageant in your head
another night of sea drift salt cod even song and dream

He dreams—

You fell in love with the fortune teller. Ignoring her gloomy pre-
dictions you looked away from every doom.
She showed you the hanged one, the drowned one, the tower—
and still you looked away.

You fell in love with the red sign that said psychic
and turned the dreamy corner.

He dreams of Lydia the innkeeper's wife
He dreams of Anke the butcher's bride.
He dreams of Serena the piano tuner's assistant.
The Sicilian weaver Maria Calvacca whom he danced with all
night once . . .
. . . a strange
a wilderness—

You imagine her in a wooden woman, a replica in wood on water.
You're infatuated with the opium addict—
she shakes her snow globe in slow motion and places it on the
mantle smiles.

Ruined kingdom.   Horse and ball   and snow
Your rockaby. He hears the women.

(even motion)

He fingers his life encased in glass now on the mantle
He shakes the globe   observes the snow   remoteness . . .
Careless dreaming wayward Steven.
(His son and daughter are all drowned)

Careless Steven drunken moody lighthouse keeper
your babies are all drowned and broken

the trojan horses made of wood and wheels and
rubber balls where children
ran and played and lost and lost . . .
Sad lullaby and lesson.

The children muffled floundered drowned and taken Steven

Sweet William floating bloated all the sea has broken moody
lighthouse memory keeper
You dream of what is past or passing or to come.

He listens to the craven and the voices of the women.

You're in love with the figure head—
carrying the missives from the shore.

You're in love with the one who says, "butterfly knot."

Sorrow drunken lonely Steven "pinned sheepshank"
holds himself and dreams   "good girl".

His wife is left his children . . .

yarn and dream and memory keeper (two fish)
flame and light heart broken weather beaten

now you wait and pray and love the most
the wooden woman on the boat.

He weeps two fish onto his plate
in longing strangeness yearning

ovoid iridescent

trembles angels angels angels of the ocean.
They ran through his hands.

the ruined kingdom

he loves across the sound the longing.
he dreams of their miraculous mooring.

You're in love with ovoid   longing   luminescent
fear no more—
(ruined kingdom   rocking
horse and ball   lapsed wing)
angels on the shore are whispering.
you strum your bleary harp and dream
you stroke your wand and weep.

Sometimes still you think about it, but you never go there any-more.

(he's been hurt he's better here)

You adore the cartographer's daughter always lost. You're taken with the milliner's sister, her felt and giddy cleaning chemical her madly laughing hatter.

You want the neurasthenic, the anorexic—blue as a water lily
the insomniac clutching her starry noctuary
the dyslexic with her backward alphabet.

You've had the fishmonger's mistress in every position
Shoulder and over again and open.

You strum your bleary harp and dream,
you stroke your wand and whisper strumpet

and weep two fish onto a platter.

You've been pinned by the beautiful mermaid's flipper
lowering a rope—(the bloated children)

It takes its toll.

You're in love with the crazy white-haired girl. She's sewing poems into her sleeve, they read: "dreamy lighthouse keeper mild Steven."

even motion.

It takes its toll.
"Celeste-Martine!" you call.

Flushed by the light of the lighthouse Steven
Is that the foghorn or the women conjured near and round and
even?

You sit gazing out in wait for the shipbuilder's niece
the sea captain's widow, the gardener's youngest daughter
delphiniums in her hair
two blue delphiniums on the sea's horizon

she loves you,
she loves you not.

The gardener's youngest daughter giggles knows a secret:
(to take a fish and put it in the hole before you plant)

and meanwhile from the peninsula of women
he hears the women sighing "oyster" "Carmelite."
in another time: 1988 or 1995

and he's rocked by sights of the women and he's taken out tonight
by the women
oh!

Across the sound the longing fear no more,
he hears in him the wailing of the women over water.
a modern Sodom and Gomorrah.
Though he's retreated 200 years or so
intimations phrases memories

fragments sometimes reach him still
oh and honey, hidey-ho, and
oh and slow   "bisexual triathlete"

Solitary lighthouse keeper lover of all women:
mermaids sirens Courtney Love and PJ Harvey even
he's dazed and stoned and dizzied

Steven often
Steven hasten
Hearken Steven open leaven
Dream your dream the sails are open

Clutching the whale watcher's guide you wait your whole life.
You dream of a mermaid: ovoid, opalescent, a lunate tail
Gorgeous, glisten, holy water basin.

You found two fish in their open mouths the wee ones drowned.
The wee ones broken
the waves and wind and sorrow Steven
sorrow over sorrow Steven
sweet William floating bloated over
sweet daughter Amy floating bloated
all the sea has taken Steven
(his wife is left, the babies are all drowned and over.)

He'd wait indefinitely for the lighthouse keeper's daughter.

he says his matins
he says his matins

and sees a figurehead through fog—and prays,
and waves *hello, hello, hello*

The insomniac's in love with the night with the stars not you
the moon's eclipse not you though you'd like to be her other lover

And he strokes to the sound of the light and the open
the stroke of the light and the winter roses and he
strokes to the sound of the women's voices

dreaming   fevered

He looks out: tall spars of sloops, ketches, and yawls
punctuate the harbor saying

over over over

he hears the rockaby and suck.

And he removes the straps, the bodice girdle a dazzling harlot
digs her heels into his back and howl

to reach the perfect sigh and guide me
risen leaven even crave.
And drowned and driven.

In masturbation
in private creation

he shifts his attention the motion
of his mind just slightly the waves and wind and sorrow yarrow

he hears two women wand and wail

even motion

even motion

"over there"
swung over there a leg
"good, it's—

it's good that way . . . "

for ultimum
for maximum for—

even motion

ovoid tail—fishmonger's . . .
opalescent thighs "it's good."

and drowned and driven craven

And put the rope around his neck and
strokes and tightens pulls and sighs—
stroke and pull:
stationmaster's wife
sea captain's widow
the gardener's plucky younger daughter

shoulder—oh and
over   open

the astronomer's assistant precision
compass circumference on her back and turned

inside a globe and snow a rope and the women begging
for fish in their mouths like
like—
drowned ones.
fish then—
a butcher's hook
A wail.
fishmonger's bitch—

he guides himself into them one by one

melancholy lighthouse keeper.
you weep two mouths onto a platter.

and sing your rockaby

dreaming Steven.

And you are watching your happiness now (hollow) float out on
the impossibly smooth sound. And for a long while it seems to be
barely moving—
until it is quite suddenly out of reach.

a figurehead through fog

You've become acquainted with the one-legged woman, the tim-
ber toe, recently—only of late—
only as of late.

You wave.

You've become acquainted with the woman deranged made of words the white haired poet madly sewing

she writes: "you can't live here any longer."

And the opium addict leaving her snowy globe once more now on the mantle

She whispers, *destiny*

she says, *follow your star* . . .

having fucked the fishmonger's mistress all night

having kissed the poet

turning—

you weep.

"good-bye knot"

having plucked the gardener's younger daughter—

she loves you
she loves you not.

Lulled by the light of the lighthouse
lilting dwindling fading world

she loves you not.

You can't live here any longer Steven and so you go.

Steven stop your weeping, your grieving season now is done
The rope is looped, the noose is hung . . . The woman of wood
recedes—
and is gone.

You say your matins.
You say your matins.

THE CHANGING ROOM

In the beach house, in the bathing hut the cabana—the secret, the sexual—in the beach house, in the changing room near the water, the couple makes love at the edge of the fog, in the just March, in some of their clothes, and she says: "I like your striped shirt," and he smiles. It is nearly their birthday and the fog is outside, the car lights light the way, and the battery slowly drains, while they—while the couple makes love and the car, their clandestine, their secret, and no one can know, no one is supposed to know. And she saunters out and the girls giggle: "we know where you've been," and she says in her sing song: "oh no you don't." She's left her lipstick all over him and the little boys shout: "Oh Romeo!" And the forbidden man winks. And the forbidden woman adjusts her lipstick, and studies the fog she screamed into and she says: "must have been an angel," and she says: "you are handsome," as he disappears down the path. And she thinks: "striped shirt" and she closes her eyes and pictures the flags of summer. And the man somewhere far off says: "Would you happen to have—would you happen—would you happen to have—

jumper cables?" And the fog takes the car. And the fog takes the shack. And the scream. Takes everything back. And they rise from the bed, after making gentle—"you are gentle"—love, and give themselves back.

Anju flying streamers after

On the nighttable: a pomegranate . . . magically.

A murmur. A murmuring . . .

"you are gentle"

The sacred river filling us.

Raising my mouth from the feast of the woman's body I see: a pomegranate

"It's like magic."

gleaming

And a woman in veils, ripe, reaching for it.

She smiles slightly, shyly whispers like a river, and says she is called Anju.

Anju—the woman who reaches, fleeing.

In the lush heat of the room—looking up from the feast of the woman's body I see: dressed in veils and glisten, whirling now—Anju

As if by magic

through desire and veils

longing without end

Silty   river   vision   burning

burning of—

the swollen river calling

through veils—a murmuring

Burning of bodies

Petals floating down

You find her in Bangkok. In Sydney. Seventeen years . . . She is in Calcutta. In Calcutta she dies.

This burning of bodies.

This motion. Anju whirling.

She belongs to whoever wants her.

Whoever wants her has her, you imagine. But not you. Through veils. O never you. Silty, silken river valley. Precious delta. Warm waters of the delta. Lie her down on the sacred bed.

And the rain—incessant . . .

We make a line in vermilion marking where the swollen river flooded.

I wish I were you coming here for the first time with the rains.

The swollen river clinging.

Lifting my head from the festival of the woman's body: Anju whirling streamers flying.

Raising my silken, gleaming, having pleasured and been pleasured, satiated for the moment at least, in this little seaside town off season, I picture:

fire   pomegranate   sweet apple   succulent

fragrant blossoms Anju

incandescent in desire come   shy one

here, Why don't you come   shy one

here   bliss   wish,

bells tinkling. You are lovely really. Bells . . . sound of bells.

Trying to get there. Trying to get to you. Sweet streamers flying
fire

A sweet taste—and around your ankles, bells.

As we approach the holy city . . . smouldering . . .

O beauteous one—how we go up like brightly colored paper, in
flames.

Opium of wings.   desire.

Lifting my head from the succulent body of the woman delirious:

catch sweet fire:
Anju
like the sweet apple . . .

And she carrying her red banner

And looking up I see through veils and veils of mad desire:

the hanging gardens
a grove of mangoes
blooming breasts and thighs
a pomegranate. Like magic.

And Anju. A sweet taste.

I feed off your fingers.
you feed off my fingers.

I lick the bone of your ankle.

I lick the bone of your ankle, jangling, o beauteous one—if you'd
let me . . .

Stay awhile.

Anju giggling hope elusive stay awhile.

Dancing, fleeting—and I returned to the lover's bed, lowering my
head

opening   smouldering

Winged and singing

The boat is waiting . . . And the black car, the Lancia, circling

circling

"Finish up now."
"Can't."
"Can."
"Don't want to."

Like magic.
The camera I reach for to photograph her produces a whirl, a blur of birds:
Anju twirling.

Reaching for a persimmon. For a—

Anju jingles as she passes. As she smiles shyly sighs a thousand birds releases.

"It's like magic."

Rain. It's raining over Bengal . . . An ocean . . .

Flooding, whirl and blur: Anju twirling

she's so far . . .

Kabir asks: "Who do we spend our whole lives loving?"

Reaching for the persimmon. Spitting out the pits.

"It's like magic."

Rain.
Another storm over the Bengal.
The sound of rain over sleep.
The voices are like breaths of coolness, gentle murmurs.

. . . rain . . .
. . . yes . . .
. . . cool . . .

That murmur? The Ganges?
Yes.

That light?
The monsoon.

. . . no wind . . .
. . . it will break over Bengal . . .

The smell of flowers.

And Anju . . . like a painting. "You're like a painting. Or a sculpture, yes . . . "

Like a child clasping a small bird.

Come here. What is that sound?

flooding   monsoon   flock of birds

She holds a cricket cage. Anju chirping. Anju singing. Anju gulping, laughing. Anju stay a moment—wait. Wait—

Anju flying streamers after

Our infinite fire. Our burning thighs. Sighs   sighs

You put a cool rag on my head
I put a cool rag on your head
In blistered fever
I put a wet salve in your mouth. You suck on it.

You suck on the wet, my fingers so close to your mouth

Your mouth . . .

And we wait for the fever to subside,

O Anju—

Row me across to the other side.

Row me across now to the other side—

She points and I lift my head: "Look, the traveling players."

with their nine mysteries. Their songs. Their copper pots of
saffron and sandalwood and mango and lotus blossom. Their box
of pigments. Their makeshift wooden bridge.

Spinning flowers out of glass

a gazelle . . .

My red dipped tongue there

My red dipped tongue there deep in the body of a woman, gathering pigment, making pictures. I draw a gazelle. A cricket cage. And Anju visions delirious. On her upper thigh I paint a gazelle in blood.

The nine mysteries of desire.

Look, the traveling players have arrived—with their oblivion books and their sixty-nine positions:

My mouth on your feet now making pictures, Anju, Anju

How much I want you   My mouth on your, my mouth, my—

Like the blind woman threading the needle, *patience,* you whisper . . .

You braid my hair.
I braid your hair.

Pulling it tightly from your head.
Pulling it tightly from my head.

How you braid and unbraid me.

How you milk me like a goat. Nuzzle me like a gazelle—in some life . . .

And the traveling players

Anju flying, hiking, Anju bungee jumping—in some life, and
Stay awhile.

The beginning of Fall brings pomegranates, she whispers. Persephone eats them before she returns to be the one who has been
waiting for her next to the violet colored river.

She smiles.

my red fingers dipped making pictures.

The full moon of your mouth o!

Your brown fingers, your long, brown fingers and the white of
your fingernails—turning red as you pleasure yourself I imagine—
Your long brown fingers, pleasuring yourself on the full moon of
my mouth

fertile, salted, gorgeous one

I'd like to paint you pictures

                 pictures of your mouth and
                 pictures of your murmuring, sighs, gulps
                 and the goddess—

painting slowly, slowly up your legs

I'd like to paint you with—

burning barge

I'd like to—

And the henna.
You're making me wild. You're making me fire.

Your sacred mound   mounted   and you're making me wild.

You open like a fan, like a flower, like a bell—

on my leg, on my mouth, on my hand, on my back, gazelle, in
some life

And the traveling players now with their thousand dreams, their
dramas, sighs, instructions—read from *The Fifth Book of Desire.*

how I feed off your fingers

burning

how you braid and unbraid me

how you milk me like a goat

sweet milk dripping, coating me

trickling dripping down my neck

lost in your folds—in some life—

Anju flying streamers after

When I get up from the festival of another woman's body: there is Anju,

waving a red banner

"striped shirt"

Pull of Anju lifting   sucking   gulping
rising from the luscious feast of a young woman's body—I'm seeing things:

how far you put your fingers into your mouth when you eat.

Anju laughing bells and

imagining

having eaten and drunk from her, having entered in every way,
having sucked, looking up:

like the sweet apple, Anju—pull of you, dream of you, desire.

Anju gasping beauty

Anju burning

Anju swaying, incense, all is sweetness, vast impermanence
and urgent

hurry!

sumptuous lascivious insouciance and beauty.

All is smoke impermanence and

Beauty.

All is Anju banners flying wild reaching

I put my fingers down your throat
     touch the
small songbird at the center of you
     trembling
at the center of you
     beating, madly
trilling whirling wait awhile—

a bowl of water where flowers float

Where I feel you now beginning to
     deep inside
     and trembling

sing and hum

deep inside   vibrate sing and hum

     toward our lives
pulled toward our night home   trembling

The nine jewels jewels

beauty—
   my own life
trembling
   flying streamers after

and the black Lancia, turned into a hearse,

and waving

life

How you braid and unbraid

want

Wanting you Anju life enlightened flying all is fire vibrate ending

pulled toward

want

I feed off your fingers
You feed off my fingers

want

The sadness of trains. The sadness of Anju there and me—

How far away you are . . . from me . . .

"just one night."

The moonstones rising in her fingernails   glowing   dark one

Coming off the light of another woman's body in bed, in the little seaside, blinded:

your holy of holies
sacred rituals
flowers in a bowl
beautiful bare feet
and the fruit
cross-legged

and your breasts—
cup of milk
cup of mysterious universe.

Your cup of milk. Your veils. How you cover your face to hide your desire. Your hand over your mouth. How you cover your mouth—

"just one night."

How you place your fingers at the back of your throat   trembling

Ringing of hand bells, finger cymbals. Play your music

Chanting Anju

Your cup of—

Play your music in me o play your music

your finger cymbals, belled breasts
the nine jewels of your tongue

in me.

Anju dances, hops on one foot, smiles, waves—

It's my mother Asha Lata's birthday today. She has long black-gray
hair that always smells of coconut oil.

And now appearing just at the top of the hill—with their scrolls
and masks and saffrons and wings (made of paraffin) and drums—
the traveling players.

Following the gleam of her body up the dark path to greet them.

The gleam of she:

she
is light and dark
she
is salty and sweet
she

she, she . . .

the light of she, guiding us now up the mountain path

she is light and darkness she is salt and sweetness she is, she is—
and I am calling after her, having glimpsed

this motion of the alphabet
this winding path of desire
moonlit
circular path of desire

finger cymbals

circular motion

Having glimpsed—

And I am calling after her as the air thins, "Anju, I have seen your
body at the Met!"

And she is calling back in what for the first time sounds like a
British accent, *Yes!*

Small ankles and wrists and waist. Blooming breasts and hips, on
the goddess.

On the goddess

In the Metropolitan Museum of Art one summer afternoon

long ago.

I remember

She took me to see the Indian goddesses at the Met that summer long ago now. Arms lifted. Finger cymbals. Leg raised. Lotus flower opening and she—so like them. Small wrists. Blooming thighs and breasts. So very much the body of a goddess—though she had not yet taken her clothes off for me. Shy one. Though she was Hungarian Russian Jewish, though she in the end would never be mine (stay a little)—never be (stay) she belonged to the universe, utter, utter,

loveliness. . .

I remember that same summer. She took me to see the glass flowers, and how she opened fragile under my hand but forget—

forget this—try to forget.

This fragile, breaking, and then broken heart. This utter pain and loveliness

delight

because there are many lives . . . Now when we see each other on the street up near the museum we smile and wave—she cradling a baby and smiling—because there are many lives and

Anju—how you recall her mirror her and I am staring into gorgeous duplication, amplification, reiteration

Back at this little seaside town having raised myself from the beach of another woman's body—

From the trance of her,

You opening in my brain like a flower, a product of desire, this woman, salty, bleeding now in the little town off season wow

I see her through veiled light

from afar.

And whirling

because there are many lives.

Anju brilliant dahlia flying petals floating after

as I lower my head

river . . .
gloating . . .

. . . and the reed boat

chimed lives—charmed living   floating

ring you like a bell
ring you from inside like a bell.

And bathe you. Anju I'd like to bathe you in turmeric until you glow gold.

Braid and unbraid you.

crouching there like that

pomegranate

round motion of the mango   sweet apple

motion of the alphabet.

We'll feast.

Ripe girls. So ready   heavy   lovely lovely

succulent

because we can't have each other
because we can't have
we dip our hands
because we can't have each other

She dips her hand in paraffin.

O Anju . . .

Dip me in your juices
your cup of sweet milk   dribbling down
your nectar

I'll taste you through your veils. Eat you   suck you   through
your veils.

petals floating
down

petals floating in a barrel

chanting, chanting
weaving slurring bobbing

Maybe just a little.

And then your fingers pressed to your forehead in prayer.

Crouched over
Coins in a silver dish.
How you cover your face now.
How you sit with legs crossed and I can see, through
veils and smoke, through—

your ripe, your wet—wanting you through—

You take my fingers and press them

To your forehead in prayer.

You move my fingers then into your mouth
pressed into your mouth
You take me in

luminous, translucent, trembling
bodies—
in prayer.

Small opening songbird and the vibrating

throat.

My fingers

you weep at temptation   ring you like a bell

In want.

And climbing the walls.

Where she undresses now slowly veil by veil

and I hear bells.

And we're climbing the walls

And we're climbing the throbbing walls and the full moon opening like a white, night blooming flower on her mouth in this little seaside town off season and the woman smiles says tell me more about this Anju

"Tell me another Anju story."

And I smile and I—

because we can't have each other yet

Anju fleeing—shy girl

fleeting life—how soon we are ashes

How fast you go

How hard to hold so small and light so—

And now the smell of almonds
and a thousand fireflies.

The small light you carry within. Waiting and waiting as you did
then, just a child—for the traveling players to arrive.

Holding in the night your small flame

and remembering—

Streamers flying after

We go up quickly like brightly colored paper chanting

Grinding in a clay pot, in a golden urn. I squat over the small
bowl, flame of you and grind, licking greedily the inside of your
smooth, delicious

cup.

Small songbird and Anju chanting flies. My ancient, my succulent
tooth hen

my honey nut. Your sacred honey nut, your sweet nectar dripping down my face my neck my back my breasts—in some life.

Anju laughing streaming honey . . .

"tell me more now,"

Gleaming, sweaty sucked through veils, she warbles sings a warbling song

"tell me more," the woman whispers.

Where we squat
desire makes a flame
grinding

in a clay pot
in a golden urn

We can do a little, Anju smiles

her smell of jasmine.
her smell of tigers.

Of earth carrying her urn, her orb, her cricket cage, her globe. Carrying her basket of charms, her bee balm, her paraffin,

Anju let me lavish you. Relish you. Chutney, ointments, ravage you

End at last our long period of fasting.

Sighing you. And flying.

Stay awhile.
Vindaloo you.
Ring you like a bell.

Gasping singing Sighing screaming looking up   desire   seaside
woman   loving   delta/woman/life, I see:

sexual energy propels the sentence looking up from the red festival
of the woman's body: Anju. Her vermillion, her inky black and
paraffin trying, trying to near you, trying to—her body disorders
how you—

play those finger cymbals now vermillion

looking up from the dipped in paraffin—on the insides of her
fleshy, petals, thighs, persimmon

looking up: Anju. Carrying the red banner.

hennaed in blood up to the wrist   gorgeous

Place me in your urn. Dip me in your paraffin. Burn.

A black Lancia is speeding along the road to Chandernagore . . .

In a past life . . .

You stood on a bridge. I was with my sister. She saw you too. A beautiful woman, just like you—she looked exactly like you, and in white, always in white. You were dipping your hands into the sacred river and weeping. You could see too much and it frightened us.

Are you sure it was I? standing on the bridge (the traveling players listen) hushed then nod

Yes, I'm sure.

The traveling players with their ladle of stars, their scaffolding, their mirrors, their charms, their hopeless plots, their horoscopes

Anju smiles sadly. *You were as filled with desire then as you are now. Does it ever end?*

In the darkened theater of our desire the traveling players construct out of balsa wood—wings.

And hold their bright threads of story—

weaving water sacred open

A tune between the two wars, "India Song," is played slowly on the piano. It is played right through, to cover the time—always long—that it takes the audience, or the reader, to emerge from the ordinary world they are in when the performance or book begins.

India song. Still

Still

And now it ends.

Now it is repeated, farther away than the first time, as if it were being played elsewhere.

What do we spend our whole lives forgetting?

She lowers her dark eyes. She holds a white flower, flame. Her wish: to live and not to hurt anyone. Sweet gazelle. She dreams. She's got a hundred schemes and plans. She's going to raise goats and make cheese and go to France, she's going to sell space on a map, and with that money she's going to buy land in the American west, and she's going to—

And she's an amateur astrologer she says. And she tells me about the bone-stars

And she's going to—

And she will—

And she will—

And I want
And I want

Cups of *chai*

my mother's maroon-colored sari with
the silver border . . .

The flower festival.

And I am going to—

Anju desiring everything, and the way her hands move through
space as she speaks making beautiful shapes

When I was a woman in white in white on a bridge in India and
you were a girl of thirteen with your sister

because there are many lives

remembering the pleasure gardens
(petals floating down)

You make a sound like no other.
And Anju spins way; Anju whirls.

Anju whirls away.

All of our lives murmuring whirling out of reach.

Have you seen the film *India Song?*

She stops whirling for a moment (shyly)
No.

It's very beautiful, yes.

The sacred river passing through us.

Sadness passing through us.

She tells me a story of when she was walking with her sister. They stopped at the bridge. I was dipping my hands into the sacred waters. *Neither of us has ever forgotten you.*

I weep. At the shock of recognition, cry. Crying, trying to call back that life. "Yes, of course," I whisper.

She is twenty-six now. She asks what were you doing—who were you loving when you were twenty-six?

The veil of memory.

We went to see the glass flowers. We went to see the goddess at the Met.

you were showing me your body shy one   it was your way as if by introduction—You showed me your body. At the Met. So like yours.

small bones
blooming thighs
and breasts

Sacred body Anju oiled trembling in the white room of my body, wrapped in yards of muslin, gauze, the arch and light

climbing the walls, and the glass flowers

the mysterious, the miraculous of our lives

"I have seen your body at the Met."

She blushes. And I describe it to her in loving, in every curve and trembling, in clavicle and dancing.

Anju blushing giggling burbling

She offers me a necklace of nuts and seeds dipped in gold and blessed in the sacred Ganges

The river passing through us murmuring

I have seen your body . . .

The sacred river filling us

And now lolling on the hillside: the traveling players.

She scampers like a child, gambols like a dancing nymph, I'm begging let me lavish you—vindaloo and chutney you grind and ginger honey you—

far deep in your—

Let me feed off your fingers

feverish

I'm begging you Anju. Her sari flung, her veil. The way when you
eat you put your hand far into your mouth . . .

Let me rub mustard oil and camphor on your chest
when you are feverish

feed you from a droplet
put a cool cloth on your head.

ground with ginger and honey

pounding the dirt floor
pounding the floor

please

Let me play your flute awhile—your fluted instrument so delicate,
fluted fanned holding my mouth just so. My breath blowing
through an opening—flowering with sound   just so

Let me blow on your small flame enlarging—

And a flock of birds disperse

A flock of birds flowering free

tin box of ashes   spices   ground with ginger and honey

rub mustard

The drug of your body   salt and sweet   the drug of your
flesh   the opium of your touch   forgetfulness   oblivion

gorgeous   obliteration   lilting

ground to a fine powder—

spice traders

and the river overflowing

You find her in Peking

Then in Mandalay.
In Bangkok.
Rangoon. Sydney.
Lahore.
Seventeen years.
You find her in Calcutta.
In Calcutta
She dies.

the forgetfulness of your touch

and the rains. And the relentless rains.
. . . ripe

She's so ripe. And shy: rub mustard

I've got an idea:

I will place the mango between your legs shy one and slowly eat so
you can see—

And then a dark plum next, and then—until . . .

my hair on your thigh   my breath   the sound of sucking

devour

And then—until—and if you'd like then you can do the same
with me my sweet you'll suck and let the juices run and

beg

desire deranging—

she goes to wanting finding streamers haze of incense haze of lilting laughing bells and veils and ringing throbbing on the way to
blooming buoyant swollen craving, path to you, path to you, path
to you—moment only, Anju, Anju—

Yes, come here, and streamers flying   how quickly   deranged by
desire

Looking up from the brilliant blinding need of another
woman's body now—

Looking up from the scarlet from the swelling buoyant salty
lovely—

body of a woman
roundness of a woman
I see in my desire:

a persimmon next to the bed and then for an instant and then for
the briefest moment glowing—a woman in sari, veils and holding
a red banner and whispering—

Yes and streamers flying

Who is it we spend our whole lives loving?

We looking that afternoon under glass at the glass flowers our

hearts already breaking—

Stay.

Sweetness for awhile.

And we will feast on one another. And we will not hurt each other
anymore I promise and honey and sweet water

the ripe mouth   the dreaming head   the hand caressing the
breast

the hand writing pomegranate on the bed sheet in blood to
prolong this delicious

The hand writing: *stay*

like magic

. . . like the sweet apple

Anju floating, Anju buoyant, Anju fleeing out of reach

. . . like the sweet apple
Like the sweetest of apples—or the persimmon.

Earthen gorgeous

fine powder

squat   grinding

ginger in a small dish   and my hand from behind

I lick your fingers clean
I lick the inside of the small dish
I lick the rim of the dish and her fingers

double-jointed crawl

underneath her   and the cool alabaster floors this time

And the glass flowers—

Her body like the body of the Indian goddesses at the Met. I have not forgotten. Now you pass with an infant and wave

like smoke

like streamers flying

and the baby now at your breast you pass, waving.

remembering.

I carry your wave within me like incense. I carry your body in mine—still

through veils

layered many lives

Still . . . in another life we might—

In another life we might have

Anju sighs kisses me on the neck, *We have never forgotten you.*

Through veils and veils of want   desire

Perhaps what she did behind those walls . . .

And my hand dipping and dipping into the clear, fierce, pure bowl
of you.

fragrant blossoms   bowl of you

As I feed you one ripe mango after another   one bright mango
then one dark plum

I feel your heart beating. The walls of your body

Perhaps what they did behind that wall was music

Anju hugging moonlight bouncing   up and down

The walls   vulva

up and down

Perhaps what they did (legs entwined, petals floating down and
blooming mouth and succulent—gasping, sighing and hands—
hovering above the glass flowers) was music.

And Miribai says:
Within the body are gardens,
rare flowers, peacocks, the inner Music;
within the body a lake of bliss,

on it the white soul-swans take their joy.

"It's like magic."

Anju whose body I have seen in a museum. Anju whose hips . . .
Anju who whispers *wings* remembering
Anju, whose heart I've heard beating
Anju, jingling as she walks, releasing birds
Anju running so as to catch the wind in her pinwheel, laughing
tangled veils.

the motion of the fan.
the motion of my mouth on her—

Anju chirping
Anju singing chanting
Anju sighing
Anju stay a moment, while.

cricket cage   and the heat

the motion of the fan and the roundness of her breasts on my—

oblivion, oblivion, o beauteous one.

and how we marvelled at the sudden sweet breeze in the room

after the torrential rains: that is how it is raining our first night.
You flooding me.

eating lotus petals—a dangerous passion.

an alabaster floor   cool   and the chandeliers
chiming and bells—its ghostly glass flowers hovering—above us.

and your body underneath   on the cool smooth

blooming   free

its pendulous—its pendulums—

This is how I would like to die then,   under a plum tree,   and
without veils.

eating lotus petals

your pendulous

steady   back and forth

your pendulous—

I have seen your body at the Met

succulent

Spice traders—

Stirring you up

I unveil and unveil you

don't be shy

eating petal blossoms

lotus position

feverish

Your safe of jewels   moonstones   rings

I watch you wrap and unwrap
your necklace of flowers
around your small wrist

Perhaps what they did behind that screen (sighs, bells, gulps,
finger cymbals, incense) was music.

pressed against a mat of leaves

on your pliant drum
with the tips of my fingers

tinkling of bells   drifting . . .

You rise:

no more exquisite obedient creature

You howl:

under a plum tree, without veils.

And we write it on the sheet with our bodies

And we make love in

your flood

—until the garden's washed away
—until the house is washed away—until the land—

Until we are ruins

washed up

in our oblivion

You put your fingers to my lips, Shhhhhh—

How fast the river erodes the land . . .

And Kabir asks, who—

and Kabir asks, who do we spend our whole lives loving?

until the garden goes
until the body
until, until—
until the world is washed away

and the lights go out
until you close your eyes

The black Lancia

until the music

I strum and unstrum you

(and the traveling players hold up a mirror and a flashlight)

gleam of you

on the harp
on the sitar

desire   bells

ankle bracelets strapped
cat's cradle tangled on your hands

Your tug and pull

how you ravel and unravel me

your choker

"a little tighter"

What is this river you wish to cross?

O honey help me get to the other side.

trance of you   trance of you

And I place a mango between us and you slowly eat until there is
only skin and pit and juice between you and me

a thin sheath

And then between my mouth and you a sheath of pomegranate
persimmon plum or peach, my sweet—and soon you'll

like the sweet apple . . . in my mouth . . . reddening

And then the only thing between

Anju Kama Sutra rising

the full moon of you

and wanting more

the cinnamon and cumin of you

your taste   like a fire
burning in my mouth

And mercy Anju put me out

strange seers and visions burning bright

take me to the river—

And the sound of paraffin

A scented bowl of water by the bed where I dip my hand. Cool compresses

And you say, *I should like to die at dusk alone under a plum tree and without veils*

desiring earth   desiring ash   oblivion, and you—freedom.

And you—peace.

Steam rising over the heart of India.

And you—Anju

Kama Sutra Anju rising

(the traveling players holding a globe)

And you—

Like the discovery of fire, like the invention of electricity, like the first glimpse of the new world, having lain eyes on—having touched—

My hand burning on your thigh, catching fire, stinging, throbbing heat of you.

the spices of your body

your infinite fire—

the river in flames

At four in the morning, sometimes, sleep comes.

And she is back again like magic. And the glass flowers, right here—in this little seaside town.

reminded by the fragile or the streamers, persimmons on a night table—or pomegranates, as I look up from the sumptuous beautiful body of another woman what, what am I remembering?

Wanting you in this life—and all lives.

Without veils, where we might rest

Where the plum tree? The burning barge? And the swollen river calling.

Dipping my hands, dipping my head

wing imprints . . . the imprint of wings . . .

Wanting you in this life finally—too late—

I am standing on a bridge over the sacred river—of course, and I am dipping my hands

I trace the place on your back—wings.

I put a cool rag on your head.

You put a cool rag on my head.
And we pray for the fever to subside.

Row me across to the other side

One is reminded of a bridge and woman on it, mourning the loss of—

Play your finger cymbals in me

Memories of long nights of love long ago

What departures do I play out, in these myriad beds?

What reunions? What elaborate overtures?

Her wave like smoke and Anju flying

So many nights of love . . .

What life do you call up in me now fleeting stay awhile. Here at the edge of this sacred river where I dip my hands

Your songs, bells, small fragrant flame, stay.

I circle the bone of your ankle.

I circle—a woman fading as she waves from the other side of the street—once you thought this would never fade, recede, or go.

scent of you, bliss and wish—wish of you—rising from your fruity
body miss—I miss you

Your body will exist at the Met for one million years

And the traveling players smiling a little sadly and waving good-
bye.

Perhaps what they did in front of that screen (and behind it) was a
kind of irresistible music.

Coins in a silver dish.

Perhaps what they did in that eternity of flowers,

faced with that delirium of petals floating down, oblivion . . .

was music.

And Sappho lifting her lyre sings:

. . . like the sweet apple
that has reddened
at the top of the tree,
at the top of the topmost bough
and the apple-pickers
missed it there—no, not missed, so much
as could not touch . . .

You ask me to strum the lyre all night

a million years ago

in which I am standing in my father's house.
in which I am standing in my father's dark house

counting beads
before the flood
before the deluge

a girl of twelve years   or thirteen   ripe

you are walking with walking stick dressed in white
toward the bridge where I beg to be excused from my father's dark
house—

a thousand years ago

You turn me to ash
You turn me to smoke
You turn me over and over again
Curvaceous, dangerous world

We suck the dew from your night, devouring your

cup of eternity, cup of

lifting to our lips our oblivion cup
our cup of infinite wishes
desire, streamers flying

mourning the loss of wings.

making love to you long ago in a slow moving boat

all night long ago in a slowly moving

The traveling players waving from the shore—through cupped hands shouting sweetly:

"good journey."

in ankle cuffs, in arm cuffs, in bracelets and henna, in kohl, in ointments—

tinkling of bells, drifting

I loved you all night in a reed boat, a thousand years ago.

spitting out pomegranate seeds

floating in jasmine and dark—lifting over and over the luscious cup to our mouths.

sweetness dripping down

"greedy one."

And the rains   and our cries   were music

a longing that never ends—not even if we live a thousand, thousand years our cup of dust

our unending cup of pleasure, and of regret, remembering . . .

I hear their moaning even today.

Now as you wrap your belled ankles around my waist, your legs tightly and I lower my mouth to the eternity of you And you are reminded in joy and grief of wings . . .

—until everything floods and blurs   and we forget
little by little

in the last light groping

how you braid and unbraid me

Your small flame, your genie slippers Anju. Your jewels. Your jeweled nose, labia, breasts and now looking up

red incense

from the menstrual feast of her body—from the festival—gorging, gorgeous world

red cup of mysterious universe

the jewel in your nose
the jewel in your—

crowned spiky jewels for friction and placing diamonds in the
rough for added—pearls, rubies, amethysts

for added

I hear their moans

and open

(the traveling players passing out mangoes now and feathers and
cigarette papers. Making something out of balsa wood. And painting scenery—a plum tree)

The light. Of exile.
Is she asleep?
Which one?
The white woman.
No. Resting.

How you do and undo me.
How you ravel and unravel me.

You place a mango between my legs and devour recalling   shy
one

and wings.

And you begin to sing.

You ask me to play the reed flute while you watch. You watch as my fingers cover each hole—open and close each hole. My mouth on—

You ask that as I blow I look at you—never take my eyes from you—desire

What they did behind that wall was music.

My mouth on you. You sing.

In the dark house with arches and redolent, where you ask me to cuff your ankles and wrists (I have seen them in a museum) to the bed. You have asked that I sit next to you in a chair as we remember one more time—wings.

And the traveling players and a reed boat.

And you cannot move and you think of the hanging gardens

suspended

Recalling her across the street from the museum, and we smile and wave—she cradling a baby

Fading. A woman you thought could never fade, recede, or go.

And the traveling players with their mirrors, their hanging stories suspended, their tears

In a reed boat.

Miribai says: I have lost it
　　　　　　and though anguish takes me door to door,
　　　　　　no doctor answers

　　　　　　Mira calls her Lord: O Dark One,
　　　　　　Only you can heal the pain.

I roll you cigarettes you do not smoke. I slowly lick the edge of the
brown paper while you watch. I do not stir from the chair. And
you ask me to make another.

And another.

And another.

While you watch.

I do a thorough job. And I smoke. O dark one—

And you reach

Your double joints. Your burning thighs.

Life of fire

Kama Anju Sutra fire

Anju gasping beauty

How you braid and unbraid me

Lost in the opium of your touch, lost

petals floating down

bells . . .

hand

My hand grazing your lush—your brush

Spread you like

Spread you like a brush fire

I put a cloth in your mouth and you suck it

And the rains . . .

Streamers flying sparklers writing. Across the night ebullient desire. Across the sky desire.

In the hanging gardens:

" . . . unveil me"
"please."

And now, come to an end finally—our long period of fasting.

"slowly this time."

We string one bead at a time.

I wish I were you coming here for the first time with the rains . . .

Good journey then.

Listen . . .
Ganges fishermen . . .
Musicians . . .

like magic

. . . something about wings

sweetness dripping down

you fluttering on my mouth

oblivion

the sound of bells

and our rituals of mangoes and music

at the sacred river's edge we beg

Blooming thighs and breasts. Cup of darkness. Cup of fragrant flowers

How quickly we go up like brightly colored paper. Like streamers

Good journey then.

Following the gleam of your body down

how you are salty and sweet
how you do and undo me—

Kashmir is a curfew zone now. Srinagar is burned down. Pahalgam, a small village about two hours north of Srinagar, is a garrison for the Indian army. When I was there ten years ago it was full of blue-eyed, black-haired rosy-cheeked Sufis standing in circles around the bank of the river. There was someone in the middle of each circle chanting. I was walking to the river with my sister Rohini, she was eleven and we passed through the huddles of men who refused to let us in to see.

Rohini wanted to find moonstones again. I think they were moonstones—clear silver-blue crystal stones—and we could just grab handfuls of the riverbed at the edge and there would be ten or eleven moonstones in each fist. The river is the clearest blue I have ever seen, almost turquoise. Late August. We feel lonely. Our parents are always drinking chai on the balcony or sleeping or reading novels or embroidering marigolds onto pieces of black cotton.

So I said to Rohini, come on. And we just started walking towards the trees. We had to come up to the riverbank and cross a bridge. Even Rohini remembers her. From a distance I thought she was a very old woman, because her hair, white-blond, was impossible. She came out of the trees and walked towards the bridge. I remember the noise of the river beneath us. She had a long knotted wooden staff in her right hand. She was wearing a loose cotton or muslin salwar—chemise—the long shift dress and baggy pants gathered at the ankles. Earth-colored like the clothes you wore at your reading. That is why I was so shocked. And her hair was white-blond, long, tied up in a very loose chignon at her nape. Do you know Princess Anne of England? Like her hair. And she had some sort of rucksack. And she was completely alone. When we reached her she looked right into our faces and smiled. How can I explain how extraordinary it was that she was walking alone in that place? I will never forget her face when she looked up. Completely present. Fearless. Peaceful. I feel like I've lived by the expression on her face, her, all this time. I've left this MFA and am now working (waitressing/selling space around a map) in order to buy my aeroplane ticket to Delhi. I want to go farther into those mountains although Kashmir is closed. My uncles are in Nepal, and this March I hope to be standing in the flower festival north of Katmandu.

Because Rohini saw her too I know that I am not remembering the woman unclearly. You look so much like her. I think I even asked you if you had ever been to India. I can see you there. There's a film by Satyajit Ray, I think it's called The Chess Players. It's the one where they were walking along the mountain paths half-submerged in the mist. It's set in Simla I think, a hill station in Himachal Pradesh, close to where I am from in Punjab. I'm Punjabi.

Fear is the only way I know what to do next. I want to write fiction. I'm scared of it. It's what I'm least comfortable with. That's why I know I should do it. It scares me to go to India. It scares me to leave something as safe as a writing program in America.

Talisman: That woman's face.

THE DEVOTIONS

One of the women thinks she glimpses for a minute through veils and veils of light, desire—

Voice 3, although it has forgotten almost everything, recognizes things as Voice 4 relates them.

Remembering the pleasure gardens . . .

remembering—she writes

could you tell me that story one more time?

"The beginning of Fall brings pomegranates. Persephone eats them before she returns to the one who has been waiting for her next to the violet-colored river."

remembering

Voices 1 and 2 are women's voices. Young.
They are linked together by a love story.

Sometimes they speak of this love, their own.
Most of the time they speak of another story. But
this other story leads back to theirs. And vice versa.

remembering . . .

prayers were painted in rice powder in courtyards, on walls, on doors.

tell me that story—

She painted the floor in front of the house each day, rising before dawn to mix the rice powder and make the paste. Every day she'd wet the floor and paint

songs of devotion
songs of mourning
songs of celebration

these fragile prayers, small messages—she paints an outer ring of trees.

kiss me.

her devotions

As the day passes, as people walk in and out of the house and the painting slowly fades

She draws in rice powder

in praise

And I right next to her now. Writing *plum, gazelle,* writing *clavicle, gazelle,* in desire's alphabet.

kiss me

glistening river

Impermanence

the way the rose clings

And we remember together the pleasure gardens again— delirious and whirling

At five in the morning she starts by beginning the outer portion of the painted prayer.

Some make art they hope will last for centuries—but this ephemeral art has no rival

Let go a little

And we draw on each other in rice powder and paste, kiss me.

remembering a little, five in the morning, the outer portion . . .

rosy, pulsing, in the pleasure gardens

sucking on a plum pit

A halo of light around our bodies . . .

the swollen flow of the river

All that was forbidden

wild

Hennaed monthly up to the wrist in blood. Marking where we
went . . .

Our daily devotions, our prayers, this disappearing art—

how quickly we go up—

And now look, the world for a moment flood-lit.

A woman on a bridge with a walking stick.

More and more often now I write to you in rice powder, kiss me,
in disappearance

drawing a small boat, a rose
a gazelle, clavicle, kiss me,
on papyrus
in rice powder

up to our wrists . . .

the flood of blood.

the swollen river overflowing

The Ganges

as the day passes, as the painting slowly changes, then fades

The plum trees . . . and how now abstracting—into a grove of hearts, it seems—or hands—in kind of slow motion, then disappears—

The way the heart clings, the eye, the way the lip clings long after

Long after

glistening river

She paints a ring of light. She paints an outer ring of plum trees.

And she imagines free. And she imagines free some day.

There's a circle of light where you walk. There's a circle of light around the whole world. She closes her eyes.

fleeting shapes   gazelles

in praise—for a moment

marking in rice the place where the river—woman—beauty

flooded

where the light.

aureole.

As we form our first words

The pulse of the . . .

The pressure of the river—the touch—

As she unbuttons, one by one

intensifying to rose

the way the elbow bends

gesture of light across—

only voices
only tremblings
possibilities

"some jumper cables"

your half turn now as you go

the press into shape
the motion of the alphabet

as if in prayer   gorgeous reiteration
stranded

a buzzing or humming

rubbing a hand on a belly as if a magic lamp

it's as if, as if—

"it's like magic"

moving the lips . . .

reading silently to himself   moving the lips over a book
as if over a woman   in awe
as if in prayer

peeling her dress off as if it were papyrus

the avalanche of her touch
falling

and a woman whispering next to a chandelier

Is that you snow ghost?

it's like magic.

slip knot
butterfly knot
pinned sheepshank
French bowline

greedy girl,

so much *dérangement*...

the Seine moving through us, still
gleaming lilting glinting
slip knot
slippery

taste of—

flex and pull and arch . . .

and the fishermen with their haul   glowing—
they look far off—

into the dazzle

I am speaking about you at last—if only to myself. I hope
not in a bad way . . .

a glance
a glimpse
in a doorway or a dawn

Is that you?

the pier, the whole world giving way

that afternoon

or a cliff

And falls into dream, on top of a woman—

rosy pearl and dawn

everything is miracle   aureole

the hills lit as if from within

intensify to rose—like magic.

Beached on the hypnotic lilting lip

Sappho conjures close what is remote to her, far off—all
want—in the place the papyrus ended or was lost or tore—
women thousands of years apart—in the lucid, orgasmic,
gorgeousness, beautiful, beautiful

Is that you?

In the city of Paris
streets syntactic
poodle basket

Filling absence

as we form our first words

Is that you snow ghost?

after making love

"Are you still carrying around your large artist's book and writing
everything down?"

only voices still—tremblings
                    pressures

her ink-stained hands

Qu'est-ce que c'est que ça?

Plum?   Star?

Sappho Sings the World Ecstatic

Beached on the hypnotic, lilting lip of a sweet—of a sweet, of a young nymph's clitoris, Sappho sings the world delirious . . . Haloed rosy—

May I say
I think no girl—

She sings, on that delicious precipice, longing, hip, the world— holds in her mouth: word and rosy pearl and world. Sweet apple. Violet breasted. Aureole . . .

May I say
I think no girl—

Between morning and afternoon, sweet apple and rosy pearl, light and light and hip and cliff and thighs. Dripping, honey, lilting, sweet, Sappho dreams hypnotic, sea, waves at her hips, between the lovely legs delirious of a gorgeous nymph. She sucks the luscious aureole, the world, she sings on that delicious precipice: *I shall go unleashed, unpegged.* The beach is wide. The world is round ecstatic.

Dizzied Sappho dreams the key in medium miraculous, following the gleam she sees a girl, a gorgeous world, a world she reaches:

On a deserted seashore a girl is being beached. It takes a long time, and instead of a back and forth motion, the waves pull only out and the tide goes visibly out. At the same time, the girl, without moving, seems higher and higher up on the shore. She watches the sea desert her with inactive longing, accepting the sand, as she dries off, which slowly collects around her. Idly she watches a bird fly long across the sky.

Says: Maya. Sappho having fallen into a fever dream and lingering. In a medium unknown at the lip of the hypnotic word and Maya, key, asleep. At the lip of the beach over a perfect woman covered. Ecstatic Sappho moans and reaches in slow motion, her hand, stranded. At the mercy of—

Bird and sea and dream ecstatic. Whispers: Maya. At the mercy of—

Maya Deren. *At Land.*

At the mercy of—

At Land. Close-up. She shudders.

At the mercy of miraculous. She conjures the woman Maya, smiles, and who is this?

On that delicious precipice, all is wonder, pearl within her grasp ecstatic. Where, oh where's my pussycat? she wonders. And watches the blond and black go at it.

Sappho longing dreams the world. She lifts her lyre and sings a gorgeous song and girl ecstatic. She holds a word, a world, a pearl, delirious. Swallow now, a sweet nymph whispers. She sighs, looks up to see a woman in a cocktail dress: crawling across a dining table on all fours toward her desire.

She smiles, swallows, stutters, mounts her like a luscious horse with bridle, saddle, leather crop and sputters *go!* And sputters *oh!* and *fuck!* She sees before her everything: a lovely curved cuneiform of woman, lilting horse and crown and wondrous girl and gallop. Frenzied, frantic: horse of her desire, live forever, oh and fuck and suck and shudder.

"Trembling was all living, living was all loving, someone was then the other one."

In the city of Paris . . .

And Sappho now is underneath, delirious. Mound and aureole and bound and ridden, shackled, and blindfolded tied reminded there of rosy world and cocktail dress and all the places yet to go. She hones her hope, her longing lust, and sung and bound by garlands, strum, encircled, galloped, sucked, she sputters—

Fuck.

At that sweet and perilous delirious. She whispers Maya Deren open mouthed, sings fuck into the lovely, lilting lyre and nymph. Delirious she holds the rosy pearl now in her mouth between her teeth and tongue and lips. Encircling the universe she licks, she laps the world ecstatic. Mouth to golden mound now, mound to mouth she sings: *May I say—*

But sucking loses her way.

May I—

And hip and Paris.

May I say—
I think no girl
that sees the sun
will ever equal you in skill.

She trembles still. She shudders, sputters *fuck* and *skill*.

Delirious and looking up from lip and clitoris and mound she sees the city of Paris lit up. "Trembling was all living, living was all loving, someone was then the other one." The women walk the street syntactic. Sing Paris Paris Paris Paris. A large white poodle dog and walking down the boulevard. Sappho longing dreams the world ecstatic.

We thought that much of what our Sappho saw was lost to us where the papyrus tore but now we see she sees the women, street, the poodle dog and even Maya crawling on the table toward her desire. Lowering herself slowly onto the woman's luscious mouth, her nymph, she lifts her lilting lyre and sings—She's seeing things: a movie screen—the beach is wide a line of white and pearls, a door. In the place where the papyrus tore. She strums her lyre and rolls her hips and shudders, sings she's seeing things:

. . . *gentle girl* . . . *sweet apple* . . . *lavish on me* . . . *with all that heaven ever meant* . . .

Sappho sings the world eternal. Each word caressed, a pearl. *Because I could not wait* . . . *Heaven* . . .

On that open mouth.

. . . *passion, yes*
. . . *utterly, can*
. . . *shall be to me*
. . . *a face*
. . . *shining back at me*

. . . beautiful
. . . indelibly

Hallucinating in the luminous afternoon, gorgeous beautiful
and skill, indelibly she's seeing things: a mouth, a key—she shifts
her hips. What is this?

Med. shot: 1st dream girl looking through window, seen
from outside (Botticelli shot).
> Road, mirror figure walking up, disappears: then
> dream girl 2 pursuing, arriving at stairs of house,
> starting up them.
> Dream girl 1 drawing key from her mouth. Her
> hand holding out the key.

Sappho lusting arches her back ecstatic.

Close up: Girl 2 trying to continue.
> Mirror figure (from below) continuing into room,
> turning to bed.
> Girl 2 trying, being tilted away.
> Top of stair, her hand grasps banister, pulls her-
> self up.
> Mirror figure deposits flower on the bed.

Close up: Girl straining up.
> Mirror figure, standing then disappears.
> Girl, as if released from pull, bounced back and
> back.
> Another position back and back.
> Another position back and back (7 shots total)
> Position forward
> Position forward
> Position forward

Position forward
Position forward
Position forward
Close up: Girl's face.

She lingers there on face and lost and sputters, hum and girl and straining up and happiness complete unleashed hypnotic.

Position forward. "She came to be happier than anybody else who was living then." Position forward. Sappho has never seen a place of such—

Girl straining up. Crawling delirious toward her desire. "She came to be happier . . . " In the gorgeous city of Paris. Poodle dog. Yellow flowered hat. Alice Babette. Sappho does not entirely understand how women appear from the strings of her lyre:

Hypnotic Maya D and others she has never seen before while on that gorgeous lilting Grecian lip and hip and nymph ecstatic.

Where is my pussycat? She watches the blond and black go at it. Closes her eyes. Lilting honey lip explore. (Papyrus tore)

Swallow now . . . and mouth and lip and skill and fuck.

Love.

Where the papyrus tore, dissolved, Sappho sings a line of sweet girls in white and gloves and veils and slippers, lilting rose, communion clothes. Sappho lying on a bed of thyme and sighing lifts her lyre. A lovely nymph caressing her from behind. Her fingers in her mouth and swallow now and suck. A garland woven around her neck. They watch the long white line of young girls openmouthed. Haloed passion aureole. So very, oh so very lovely—singing, sighing makes them so.

Once I saw a very gentle
very little
girl picking flowers.

Golden genet
grew along the shore.

And the ripe girls wore garlands.

Girls with voices like honey.

And the garlands were wild parsley . . .

Long shot: Road. Hand deposits flower, disappears.
   Shadow of girl arrives, her hand picks up flower.
   Flower dangling beside girl's legs walking.
   Girl's shadow walking, stops, smells flower . . .

Med. shot: Girl's shadow on door, hand knocks, tries
door.
   Hands get key from purse, key slips, falls.
   Feet, key dropping on ground, bouncing away.
   Hand, reaching for key, misses, key bounces
   away.
   Key bouncing down stairs.
   Key bouncing down stairs, followed by feet pursu-
   ing.

Close-up: Hand finally catching key.
   Feet going up stairs again.
   Hand with key unlocks door, pushes it open.

Pushes it open. Sappho's thighs are parted, opened by the woman 6 BC and oh and slow and fuck. A bouquet of visions flowers wild. A tender key. An open mouth. A world. . . . And they called the poodle Basket.

Sappho sings the world ecstatic. What lovely turn of mind, desire has brought this dreamy procession before her eyes. She sighs. She smiles. And the little girls in their white dresses gathering flowers.

The girls for once are not ornamental. The girls for once are not just decorative. Incidental. The girls and their gorgeous rituals and tenderness which make Sappho honey song and hum are not for once relegated to one white wing somewhere. The girls for Sappho are the whole story. Holding their delirious bouquets and visions, open-mouthed.

Sappho sings and sells sea shells. Sappho sings by the seashore. She rolls the rosy aureole and pearl the world around and round. Sea pearl to pearl with her and lip she shudders honey gold and conjures—this must be Paradise—or maybe Paris. "She came to be happier than anybody else who was alive then." Gorgeous lilting rosy pearl. She rides the women world syntactic. Sings Paris Paris Paris Paris. And they walk the poodle Basket.

The blond and black go at it. Ask Sappho finally, How about it Pussycat? Oh that delicious precipice, miraculous, delirious. And dreaming Sappho sings and weeps and shudders, stutters—a great appendage now attached! And strapped—and oh and oh and oh and oh and—

Poodle dog ecstatic!

A rosy line of girls in white communion clothes. She reaches for the key unleashed. A halo. Open door. And hip unhinged. The girls for once are the whole story. The blond and black go at it. Gallop!

Pearl to pearl to pulsing pearl she drags her tongue and teeth a little, throbbing ripe and slower, shudder. She sucks the rosy pearl ecstatic. Girly girl. She sees the sea and shoulder, slower, shells. And yellow flowers grew there gentle. She licks her salty lips and sucks eternal. The little girls all in a row—Sappho's singing makes it so.

She sees a woman now against a door (papyrus tore). Blue. Blue door. Stutters. Shudders. I adore. She crawls, adores, on all fours toward her desire. Syllable by syllable. Word by word by word.

My beauty love, Sappho dreams, adores, in the place the papyrus tore.

And Sappho sees:

Med. shot: Two girls sitting across from each other with the sea in the background.
Same shot, very still, without movement.
Face of blond talking animatedly, pan down along her arm which moves figures on chess board; hold on chess board until another hand comes in; pan up to brunette talking animatedly.
Chess board with alternate pieces being moved at rapid rhythm. Chess moves:
17 WKt–Q5
17 BQ x P
18 W B–Q6
18 B Q x R ch
19 W K–K2
19 B B x R

She marvels at the specificity of her 20 B K–Q3 desire:

Blond talking animatedly then pan to brunette talking; then pull back to show both on one side of the board leaning their heads back and as camera continues to pull back reveals her caressing hair of girls.

20 WP–K5
20 B Kt–QR3
21 W Kt x P ch

Their faces laughing, leaning back.
Her face laughing.
Over her shoulder everyone laughing, their arms reaching forward and moving chess pieces without looking.

21 B K–Q
22 W Q–B6 ch

What lovely world is this that Sappho conjures in desire? BK–Q and P–K5. Everything within her grasp. The world is vast, a pearl, hypnotic. She crawls on hands and knees toward word and world and rosy pearl and sea eternal.

Where oh where's my Pussycat? Where's my Poodle Dog? And Maya Deren on all fours. [Shot B-7.]

Sappho longs and loves the world.

And Alice Babbette, petite crevette. On the rue Christine after the war. Adore. Picking flowers gentle. Rose is a rose is a rose eternal and I am because my little dog knows me.

She wanders gorgeous key syntactic. Violet-breasted. Poodle Basket.

The Black and Blond at Chess

Suddenly, she is no longer holding the stones but is standing there watching two girls sitting over a chess board playing. They seem gay about it, talking to each other as they do so. Then she is standing in back of them, because they are suddenly both on one side of the board and she begins stroking their hair. They love it and lean their heads back like cats and begin to laugh with delight and she, stroking their hair laughs too. The chess game goes on although they do not seem to play very seriously. Nevertheless the white queen is about to be taken and as the black-haired one moves a figure to knock off the white queen, the girl suddenly stops stroking their hair, grabs the queen, and begins to run.

She grabs the queen. She pets the cat. She pets the queen. She goes unleashed. She holds the key. A rosy haloed line of girls in white begin to sing. And that of course is everything. She rolls and sucks and rosy pearl. She holds the key, the word, the world, and sings ecstatic.

You were dazzle

What filled us those nights next to the ocean besides sorrow besides rage, besides pain was—

We were sadness and rage and pain, but we were—

phosphorescence—

the slam of the ocean

iridescent

You were gorgeous,

You were wild,

And how at night we listened to the water raging and stars.
I have not forgotten

glowing flowers in a barrel
flowers filling the room and dazzle

A summer afternoon. Your designer shoes and maids. Your Henry
James. You could have anything, buy anything you wanted, you
said:

"on your stomach this time"

crawling together, making something monstrous, through the
sand.

In the ditch we were digging

or on the broken pier when you were slumming

those lustrous afternoons . . .

"guide me like a Carmelite . . . "

What filled us was rage and sorrow and hurt
The black veil of August descending and birds. Caught.
Trapped in the end. There's no way for this to work . . .

make me shudder once more

squirming under you

When you bit my lip it bled
    "go ahead."
salt and ocean and blood mixing
all the fluids of our bodies mixing
    and language

And you whisper "beg." And you whisper "fetch."

We were careless, we were sensational sex, the slam of the ocean—hallucinations:

On the beach at twilight materialized ten lifeguards to make a pyramid—I have not forgotten

The planks giving way,

The carelessness of our inflations: the pier suddenly on fire.

I wanted others and you were furious. I wanted others and you were humiliated.

The triangles you tried to negotiate.
the pyramids . . .
On a beach at dusk
we watched.

The fluorescent.   Luminescent.

Humiliated you wanted to leave me before I left you. But you were sex addicted, addicted to our bodies together. And so you kept putting it off. Angrily. Growing to despise us both.

But I would never have left you.

Our sad history. I would never have left you.

We were alive—

The phosphorescent tide.

We were gorgeous and gleaming. Ecstatic.

Ride me like a saint. Guide me like a Carmelite.

We were tangle and pull and gag but we were dazzle.
We were hurt and heartbreak and never again—

We were strung out. We were strung up.

We were head pulled back and gleaming.
We were danger. We were ruin. We were
gasping and swoon. Abandon.

   "Go ahead"
You took off my suit
bit my nipples until—
left me naked.
a small tuft—scratchy then
   "go ahead."

You could have anything you wanted.
   "beg"

You were money and sensational sex in the blaring
afternoons.

You were rage, you were beauty, you were electric and what filled us was light, what filled us was being completely alive.

phosphorescence

You who idolize power
                force
                lucidity
                definition
                rhapsodize   control
You were pompous
                grandiose
                pretentious
                competitive

I was danger, disorder.

A broken pier.

You said him or me.
Her or me.
Them or me.

I was hair pulled back.

The planks giving way under our weight, our glowing bones, your designer combat boots, your rage.

You were the consummate, you were the notorious: party girl, networker, careerist par excellence.

You were John Cheever and Henry James and Bridgehampton and
rules and regulations.

We were losing our way.

You who commemorate "found" with flags,
"there," "home," with little stickers, markers
medals, with rewards . . . You were losing your way and you were
furious.

Kiss my clavicle.

We were flowers in a barrel (it took years to end) but we were
dazzle.

Unending well of tears

We were always changing shape, a broken pier, flowers in a barrel,
flames.

We were losing our way

you who idolize strength, definition, distance and I, source of disorder, random, falling, pressed close up

"God you are gorgeous."

We were doomed but we were unstoppable dazzle.

We were lost.

We were losing.
We were the memory of survive.

Tripping down the wayward aisle. The wooden planks giving up, giving way. A hand pinned back, forbidden.

And you whisper, "good girl's knot."

We were losing our way.

And you whisper, "beg."

exquisite hour

And you kiss my clavicle once more.

We were broken and fractured and fallen into water
refracted in light—shackled
Left for dead devoured by brightness—blinded

The memory of survive. I would never have left you.
Flowers in a barrel—

We were gorgeous on that dazzling and disappearing pier we were broken, fractured, fallen into water refracted in light and sadness—dazzle—it took years to end

And tangle and pull and regret

The phosphorescent tide don't go don't end

We were strung out   We were strung up

And you whisper "don't." And you whisper "go."

We were careless, we were sensational sex, the slam of the
ocean—hallucinations:

Ride me like a saint. (Guide me like a Carmelite.)

We were tangle and pull and gag but we were dazzle.
We were hurt and heartbreak and never again

Unending well of tears

We were always changing shape, a broken pier, flowers in a
barrel, flames

We were shipwrecked   we were reckless   we were wrecked

We were pull and regret.

We were too careless.   And too careful.

We were flagrant and we were rage. Conflagration: the pier suddenly on fire. Cremations. We were ashes. We were the memory of
flowers in a barrel.

You who idolize power, money, force, definition, lucidity
control

We were lost, we were losing. We were flower petals floating in a barrel.

We were unstoppable dazzle.

We had lost our way and flames and flowers and always

changing shape.

You were flagrant, you were fury, you were fear. You were decorum and rules and all of it doomed. You were broken hearted and pier on fire

You were never again

And you were dazzle.

Exquisite hour

Is that you snow ghost? Is that you candy gram? Strange visitations . . .

White moves in no particular order. Or patterned on things we can have little idea of—cancelling the landscape, negating the landscape, isolation. Is that you? A sky so white . . . delirious . . .

This is your Exquisite Hour.

You are the isolate, beautiful like that, with your indolence, waywardness—desultory—clutching a snow globe and a rabbit. Fugitive.

The avalanche of your touch, as we fall into your blizzard. Is it safe there?

Don't make me laugh.

And remembering is like falling some. Yes, you were the noviate, the fugitive—exquisite. Oh yes.

And he leads her through the stages of her remoteness hoping, hoping, out of selfishness perhaps, that she'll come back now if only for a moment. Her white out. Her blur. She flickers on. Flickers off. Is that you snow ghost . . . Sucking on a candy numb. Falling. He rose beneath her tongue.

Voice 3, although it has forgotten almost everything, recognizes things as Voice 4 relates them. Voice 4 doesn't tell it anything it didn't know before. There was a time when it too knew the story very well . . .

. . . tell me about the pearls again.

she liked to place a few pearls in his condom.

really did she?

and later one by one—she strung them.

oh?

Mindlessly even now as she listens she slips one or two into her dreamy mouth, trying to remember. O forgetfulness, as the snow . . .

She whispers *maitre.* She's no match for him. And he says *angel eyes,* as the drug sucks the world back from her.

Must have been an angel . . .

The eerie glow of the snow. She strung them. Sweet and numb—beneath her tongue.

She slips.

And the world dims.

And the world low-lit.

Until you can scarcely remember

scarcely—scarcely

And you let that place open in you—like a blinding white bloom—gardenia, behind the ear of that woman, that—

God that velvet voice astray—

astride you now—

You swerve with her into forgetfulness or carelessness—or something—

In our ice house. God, it's gorgeous here as you watch space enter you, take you now in its embrace—let everything slide. Is that you—fill up with white—How everything—

irreversible you've heard—a distant world fills up with white.

The eerie glow of the snow. White moves in no particular order. And in the light, you, gloating. Such lips. Sucking on emptiness. Until the lips and tongue are numb, until . . .

Yes, in the pleasure gardens, a beautiful music mindlessly she still slips a pearl from time to time into her dreamy mouth.

And she clutches her icy writing tablets. Her hand abstracting—every word you make dissolves now. In our ice house whispering *scarcely, scarcely.* You are driving into last late white—your Escape Club, it's lovely, *n'est-ce pas?*

And the blue tablet, once black, slips away, slides from you, *sans souci.* You're no match for it.

One hardly remembers such snow. Such silence.

A full feeling—a fulled up feeling. The white lit way. Your cloudy, luminous eyes, your cup of moon spilled night.

And she shakes her snow globe and puts it on the mantel. And she smiles wreathed in freezing fog. How soft now the edges are. How like smoke the trees have become.

And you love what is far. And you love what is far why not? And the snow with its induction into sleep. I know . . .

And you are hip high in snow. White world. I know you're hurting. I know a lot of things.

Her bleak atmospherics. And the remoteness calls her: *lover, beauty.* And the remoteness whispers *wrap yourself around me. Give it up.* And she retreats easily and she gives in easily. It comes naturally now. Licking the last flakes off the pane.

They say: follow your star.

Ming, is that you? Her gray cat. And doesn't it look exactly like snow has fallen on his furry paws? They say . . .

She fingers her books: slim, bleak, appreciated by only a few.

The white paper before her dissolving now—every word you write—in a kind of tearing and oblivion.

And she slips into the white of herself—into the white—her life snowing. A muffled, peaceful sound and she feels could it be? slightly aroused by the white, by the taking away finally of everything as she falls into some infinite. Voice 3 said something about pearls once. And the little girls danced all night—remember? Until their shoes were thin.

A little bit.

And she makes love to the distance as it opens inside her and she's falling. The space opening now wider and wide until it seems—and she is straddling it, and she is pulling it up inside of her or it is—the vortex swirling. The suck of the void. I know you're dizzy honey. I know.

And a voice long dead sings, *Il neige.*

You are licking the last flakes—hip high

Look, you're no match for it.

And the white moves in. Oh, *il neige* all right—your cracked snow globe left on some mantel by the sea, fuck.

You've forgotten it.

Ovoid, lunate, opalescent life—fuck.

You miss your mouth almost entirely now.

Over forty varieties of lipstick . . .

You did, you used to put pearls. A shadow self. Disaffected now. Few friends and no interests. Aimlessness.

"Why you wonder all of a sudden—why should I be—the only person to whom happiness—is absolutely forbidden?"

And when she lifts her bleary head she sees, out the window—her weird atmospherics: strange last fires of the city. *Hey.* Walking against its inferno lit up. By bonfires. Through drifts and drifts of snow and cold now hide. She lifts her notebook to her chest.

In the delirious, walled city, the voice of 3 is whispering. Fire. The fencing master in white calling *Anna, Anna, Anna* and she tiny and freezing and wrapped in the pelts of rabbits, against the fire glow. Hide.

Pushed up against the fire glow. Mouthing Anna. Offering his hand in the demolished city. Smouldering. And she is just a girl in boarding school reading by firelight. Huddled around the fire of the alphabet trembling—sure, look I know you thought it could save you—And the pages burn.

And where are they when he comes to rescue in his extinguishing whites?

Off in Zurich or Saint-Tropez, remember?

No, not really.

She's been left in the very best. The very best of boarding schools. With her French and Latin lessons very best. Her ballroom dancing. Her fencing instruction.

Her very. Yes. So why so gloomy then? Phantom daughter of snow. Clutching a box of very dark chocolates from Switzerland. A demented, bittersweet waltz step.

1—2,3   1—2,3   1—2,3

You'll try to hide in the fire garden, but he'll only find you idiot. He bellowing *Anna, Anna* for hours it seems. But it takes 43 seconds.

How does she know that?

He seems to care. Chanting *Anna, Anna,* wafting like that having detected defection, dissonance—wayward angel, little fugitive, *jardin,* come to me. And I shall tell you the story once more:

Once upon a time there was a king who had twelve daughters each more beautiful than the other.

Now the other story:

He whispers, and it's like a fairy tale: could you tell me that story once more? *My father's father's father.* Bringing silk and tea and spices. And he holds up his bleary chalice, cup of doomed universe, pale stare—silk and tea and other things. What is this Paradise he offers?

" . . . The East India Company. The Early Trade at Canton . . . "

" . . . like candy . . . "

" . . . come on . . . "

Staggering. Staggered in her subzero. In her negative numbers. The landscape cancelled. In the avalanche of his touch.

Avalanche. And doesn't the word come from the French? *Avaler.* To fall. If she could find her French dictionary. If you could find it. Once more. One more time . . .

Fuck.

The snow took our animated, vivacious friends, all.

One hardly remembers such silence. Or such snow. And she in a kind of perfection falls into drift and darkly luminous dream falling. Falling, fallen, or is it fell? The language of the other life. I look up from the page onto a field filled with newly fallen snow.

Come with me, we'll get our wings tonight.

Falling, falling snow but not yet fallen—still, unfallen but about to—it took 43 seconds to fall . . .

. . . wings tonight. Contiguous with the abyss. Brush me a thousand, thousand times.

To gifted Arab doctors eventually fell the medical legacy of the classical world, and with the inheritance came knowledge of the drug opium.

The slur of your touch. Her eyes a glacial blue. The opium of your touch. Pill box. Tiny jewel box. Candy gram. Sweet and numb. Now you suck on the stamen of a poppy. More than contented—oh yes . . . Lapsed. Tiny, ashen bridegroom in white. Tiny magi. Magic. They say: *follow your star.* They always say: *star.* All the processions. He followed her into the fire garden.

The luminous white, the gloomy torso. The glare of the torso of the fencing vest.

A white flower—desire—powder—target in the night. What the insomniac saw. The child saw. In the snow, a fire alphabet. Huddled there.

Strange last fires of the city. Walking against it, lit up by bonfires she runs for protection, remember? into the walled garden on fire where she lifts her writing tablet, wrapped in the pelts of rabbits.

No not really.

I'll make you a star, he whispers.

Champion, he whispers . . .

Masterpiece, the master whispers.

You see his whites even from this distance—and the torso's weird glow. Even from here. What one would call a mesh over the face, a kind of electric wiring through white. And a soft glove . . .

In the mirrored room he said, *bend your knees.* In the mirrored room he said, *en garde.* Hips level and shoulders. Arm away from the body. Hold the position. And he whispers delirious, *I'd like to break you in* . . . soft glove. Target.

Now beat, now beat again, now counterbeat, extend and lunge. In the luminous, duplicated white. *Champion. Star. Give me your arm:*

She sucks on the rose between bouts, swollen with a kind of—

oh yes you do—you like it, don't you—a kind of white rain. Oh yeah, it's nice sucking like this.

I'll make you a champion. Put you in the winner's circle little girl.

You're just twelve. He feeds you something very white from his hand. A strange force enters you and you black out. Driven there. The avalanche of his touch. *Riposte,* he says and the world slips. Contiguous with the abyss. And doesn't avalanche in French—*avaler*—

Riposte, he says, but she can't seem to—the world slips—the known vocabulary—the actions that once accompanied such commands.

Long before the golden age of Muslim civilization at Baghdad, Sabean seamen were piloting their lantern-rigged craft into remote corners of the eastern seas, making regular calls at ports along the Malabar Coast and as early as 300 AD, a colony of Arab traders seems to have been established at Canton.

His father's father's father.

And you slip into the white blur of yourself—into the white—your life snowing. You lift your arm to shield yourself from the glare. Turn away. Away again.

The drift of insomnia and snow . . . Someone took our pretty, vivacious friends, all.

The fencing master leading a white horse who balks to the fire garden . . . The flare of nostrils . . . "Blindfold it." The bridle and bit, of the drug, the suck of the drug—muzzle it—"fuck"—"a tranquilizer." The use of the mute. And he forces the horse into the fire. I'd like to break you in.

Calling *Anna, Anna, Anna.* in the fugitive garden on fire. Whispering *princess, princess.*

She's crossing the river valleys—the Cardamom Hills—She's quite mad.

Bright, so bright. Shiny. Trinkets.

*You are light as a feather,
as stiff as a board.
As light as a feather . . .
As stiff as a board . . .*

Ming is that you? Sitting on her school books. The cat smuggled in—against the rules.

She enjoyed sex only once, as a school girl with another girl, one voice reminds the other now. Oh yes, that she still seems to remember . . .

Anna, Anna, Anna!

three times she feints.

three times she deceives the fencing master

Who whispers—whispering—no matter how she closes her ears to it—whispering, *destiny, destiny, masterpiece.*

Three times she escapes him.

Whispering, *princess,*

forty-three seconds my star.

Three times she denies him.

The fourth time she falters, falling. And in the target garden he finds her. In his whites. And weren't you just asking for it? Of course you were. Of course you must have been. O recklessness.

You thought you could hide behind your writing tablet poor child. The burning light of the alphabet. Studious, obedient one.

And now what have you spent your whole life crossing out in white—what?

Not all the opium in China . . .
Not all the love in the world . . .

"The heroin makes one's eyes beautiful. There is no doubt that I am attractive. I watched myself in the glass for a long time, which gave me pleasure."

This is your Exquisite Hour. A blotter of wings. Deranged waltz step—your very off-glissade. Under your tongue. Your oh so very— 1—2,3   1—2,3   1—2,3   1—2,3 . . .

And you dance out of any grasp. They say: *destiny* and *follow your star*, the last landscape neutralized. At last all the things that could never work, they say: *at last.* The Chinese puzzle box of the world—solvable, then solved at last. As of late. Snow ridden—

Snow collecting in the high walled garden. The fire finally out. In a haze of belladonna. In the burnt garden. The garden of char. The black rose of blood rising *wings tonight* and falling in the syringe. Clutching that pathetic rabbit and candy box.

The drift to the needle. *Oh yeah—*

A strange paradise enters her, invades her bloodstream, and she turns away from nostalgia, from sentiment, from fear of any kind. She turns away from his never. Taking in wings and forgetfulness—she opens inside. Falling.

His father's father:

After the bomb was released forty-three seconds passed before it found earth. Can you see it floating and falling in those last moments—not quite one minute left—my love, love. Not quite one minute left my dear. That demented, that lilting free fall—

And the bomb fell like a flower floating
for forty-three seconds

A black bloom under the tongue
forty-three seconds
a kind of slow motion . . .
last exquisite minute.

She watches August descend like a black veil. The month she
shall perish she's sure. She shakes her snowy globe—a kind of slow
motion—the writing tablet slips; the world embraced by ice.
Wings tonight.

She's looking for the syringe and she is wafting and floating and
waffling. On her mantel—the cup of mysterious universe, perfect
universe, paradise. And I too now, desirous of the night—The
fluttering hand. How the hand flutters.

She opens her mouth and devours wings. Light. Under her
tongue a dissolving universe—bright—a blotter of world, before
everything is obliterated—under her tongue like an x ray revealing
finally who she is and where she must go—slow—like a map, like
a petal, under her tongue. Hold it there. Hold still. There now.
Shhhhhh—As the forever moves in.

Does she remember the time—a blotter of wings, the pattern
the petals made—the time she made a print of the penis in vege-
table dye?

No.

That odd split head. A tattoo. A lovely pattern . . . Or the
day—does she remember stuffing butterfly wings into her mouth,
imagining motion, eating—as if she might eat motion . . . Move
again.

Parry riposte.

It is not winter as one might expect at the asylum, at the retreat
for the cessation of the abuse of narcotics; but a kind of perpetual

spring—a wide expanse of green. Making her—it always made her nauseous and dizzy—the hilly, the color she roams, homeless there. Is that you? Withdrawal?

All night you wear a gleaming pelt. Claws. It's terrifying crawling around on all fours biting. Snout to the earth. Trying to get free. All day you type a letter, go to group therapy, walk with an escort across the green.

All day you try, in vain, to subtract his image from the mirror,

The fencing master mouthing *masterpiece.*

To take his image from the mirror.

All night you wear a pelt again—and those strange marbleized eyes . . .

Look, she's no match for it.

The gorgeous dissonance of her body now as she faces and then voluntarily walks back toward the white. God, she's dying, begging for it. Wings tonight. A woman rocking on the rockaby.

Brush me a thousand, thousand times.

Never let me go.

A drug-induced abortion. "What a miserable waste." Stop the child. Stop the child. No bigger than your thumb. "What a miserable waste of happiness."

Brush me a thousand strokes. Never let me go.

"A drug induced abortion," they whisper.

"What a miserable waste . . ." Is that you snow ghost? Insomniac child.

" . . . bringing back a series of exotic fevers . . . and a white powder . . . "

" . . . she fell in love with the horsey set . . . " (clinking of glasses)

" . . . have you heard lately from Mary Burns?"

"Isn't she a little old for that dress?"

(useless chatter)

" . . . That's not Dr. Gisella Brigitte Oppenheim over there is it?"

A clinking of blue glasses sparkling.

As a child she liked to go ice skating. As a child she dreamed of going to the Ice Capades with her mother.

"Poor dear, her mother! Oh! She loathed just the *idea* of the child . . . dumping her in boarding school . . . Never going to fetch her . . . "

(useless chatter)

" . . . Dietrich Fischer-Dieskau"

You close your eyes to *Winterreise.* It's too much, too much. And he sings *A stranger I arrived, a stranger I depart again.* You yawn.

And he sings *I do not want to breathe again until the towers are out of sight.* And you disintegrate a little.

Yen, dope fiend, hop head. Tincture of—

The drift to the needle.

"have some fun."

Oh what a party.

And there's the diplomat again . . . "quite handsome."

In another life she'd like to suck him off—in another world . . .

She's still capable of surprising herself.

(A glacial smile)

" . . . acting like school girls."

Peaches in the voice and falling. It's like peaches . . . numb. Catching the peach, lifting her buttocks once—holding her cheeks in your hands and lifting. A falling feeling—school-girls . . .

. . . the use of the mute.

(glasses clinking, shards of civility)

Correct me if I'm mistaken but that seems to be, that looks an awful lot like Mr. Brilliant Chang. Eliza Bright. Professor Dog Head turning the corner now all the world lit up again. Highest purity. Their gorgeous charms and powders. Their glitter. Exquisite. Charms tonight.

Nothing but snow and ice.

The snow made us left-hearted, slowed up the ventricles. We ploughed through perfect remotelessness. We ploughed through fields—warped. Through irresistible drifts. Drifts of—we're lost.

Protected from all harm. All harm dissolved in white—hip high. As you fall from what seems now an incredible height . . . unharmed. Last flakes on the pane. Precious disappearing things. For forty-three seconds they say. To reach its target.

His father's father

You are as light as a feather.

Her mouth now smeared across the wall.

" . . . she's lovely, remote, rather serene, don't you think? smiling . . . "

"she wrote books once, you know . . . "

"really?"

"white opium smokers . . . "

" . . . the early trade at Canton . . . "

" . . . pleasure users"

The First Opium War 1839—42.

You wrap yourself around the void. The vortex swirling. A blossoming under the tongue. The snow opening. I know you're hurting badly, he says. I know you're dizzy baby, he says removing his mask. I know a lot of things.

A stranger I arrived and a stranger I depart again.

And she'd like to stuff a sock soaked with ether into the yowling mouth of Dietrich Fischer-Dieskau.

Correct me if I'm wrong but that looks exactly like . . . That seems to be—blurring, a flurry of—There were sparkles, a sparkling—glowing—a high walled garden—forty-three seconds—with fire.

The bridle. The mute.

What was I saying?

In the sensuous lexicon of falling, where I write, where I like to write, more and more often now. Charting a motion and its many permutations, its many fallings into desire, language—waywardness, hope . . .

How you just wanted to be taken away. Taken out—to become silent because there wasn't any language for this. Look you're no match. You're no match for it.

Once.

Once you walked off so far away from the person you had been. You staggered and forgot how to get back. Lost the way back.

Dancing till your shoes were thin—all the fathers watching . . . trying to catch you at it.

When you look up it's still called the earth sure. Although everything is changed. You're still called your name strange OK, OK. Dizzy, clutching a black book.

And I am drowned in smoke this time. Having left the flue closed (deliberately, then?) and I think of you Anna—trying to navigate your way through snow—looking up, the countryside suddenly wreathed in smoke and snow. Staring as if seeing fire permanently in the mind, in the eye, mesmerized by heat, by light. Delirious. And I rest my blurry pen. . . . Must have been an angel. . . .

And you are listening to a woman singing only slightly out of phase. Her voice perfected in its exhaustion, its decadance as it falls away arriving late to the party—wafting and falling. Velvet, like velvet. Wings.

"You're my thrill, you do something to me."

"he's a diplomat's diplomat . . . "

" . . . bringing silks . . . "

"You send chills right through me."

Silken—the woman with the velvet voice. Exquisite. Salvation. Lady Day.

Halo. Aureole. I lift my arm to the glare. Useless. And we're lost in her squalls—her luxurious, her gorgeous darks—*"where's my will?"* singing only slightly out of phase. And her moody accomplice holding the mute. I know you're hurtin' darlin' . . . I know you're kind of blue. Here:

Bright, So bright. Shiny. Junked up. And you move into the swerve and drag of her voice. Gardenia floating, gardenia falling. Drug and voice and flooding down are dripping. A strange paradise enters. The woman singing.

You're my thrill. Yeah, you do something to me all right.

See how they cook the opium into pearls . . .

And you bring up the woman's voice now. Push the score. So as not to get lost, not yet, oh—in the garbled warp her—God, it's beautiful here. The pier collapsing.

And the velvet woman remembers the effect of key don't change it. And he doesn't change it. His mouth on her—don't change anything oh—

But that was long ago.

She watches snow fall on the lovers in miniature now as she shakes her globe. Large, hopeless, gloating, outside.

And she watches the tiny figure put pearls—

She smiles.

At first we didn't see the movement, the beginnings of movement. But it begins at the first note of "India Song." The woman in black and the man sitting near her begin to stir. Emerge from death. Their footsteps make no sound.

They are standing up.

They are close together.

What are they doing?

They are dancing.

They are merged together in the dance, almost motionless. Now quite motionless.

Voice 2: Why are you crying?

No answer. Silence.

Once upon a time there was a king who had twelve daughters, each more beautiful than the other. They slept together in a hall where their beds stood close to one another. At night when they had gone to bed the King locked the door and bolted it. When he unlocked it in the morning, he noticed that their shoes had been danced to pieces, and nobody could explain how it happened.

And she carries her blur and releases it just before he—before— in immaculate whites. It's dangerous here. Everything on fire. She holds her rabbit pelt and book to her.

1—2,3   1—2,3

So the king sent a proclamation saying that anyone who could discover where his daughters did their dancing might choose one of them to be his wife and reign after his death.

Merged together in a dance, almost motionless.

And we savor the distance. And we savor the forest. Tasting its many darknesses. And we love what is far. And we are called to the river's eternity. The black pomegranate on the table. Our pupils dilated: *look, look, oh look!*

In which I am standing in my father's dark house
In which I am standing in my father's dark house
counting beads—before the flood—
before the deluge—a girl of twelve years.
You are as light as a feather.
Dizzy (1—2,3) now. One—two, three—

When the King put the question, "Where did my daughters dance their shoes to pieces in the night?" he answered, "dancing with twelve princes in an underground castle."

And you walk out of all enclosures, all that has confined you—

She is walking with walking stick dressed in white toward the bridge when you beg to be excused from your father's dark house

I want to go further into those mountains—though Kashmir is closed. I want fistfuls of moonstones. I want now my mother's maroon silk sari with the silver border. Her hair smelling of coconut oil. I hope to be standing soon in the flower festival north of Katmandu.

Only bells, only charms as you walk away. As I walk away from all that has kept me in place. Afraid.

Wearing on our hands our frayed dancing shoes. Discarding at last the fencing plastron, and the pelts of rabbits. The father's dark house redolent with arches. We say, *at last.*

Snow falls like music and you escape. They always say: *follow your star.* Independent, indifferent—spectral visions of the fencing master. A blur of blades. There now—there—*touché.* She finds the brilliant opening—*touché,* and walks away from his never . . .

You must have been an angel . . . All harm dissolved in white—the effect of key don't change it—hip high. Let it melt under your tongue like snow—forgetfulness . . .

I'd like a little nighttime language. I'd like a little night language—music. I need a little night now.

(Mozart playing)

" . . . the loafing class"

The glare of the snow. "Hello." You squint. You lift your arm to it.

" . . . like the awful smirks on the faces of child prostitutes."

And weren't they just asking for it?

Clutching her heart-shaped box.

Hiding in the smirking garden. Is that you snow ghost?

While he does a demented step, a kind of *flèche,* 1—2,3   1—2,3 1—2,3   1—2,3

"Oh let the child have her Ming. Poor thing."

Never

"How quickly she is out of jumper and togs. How quickly the pigtails I loved to pull—as she bent her knees then opened—now coiffed for her senior dance. She is tall, slim, high-heeled—no longer adorable. Her improbable bosom. Turning back, I remember that night when I finally found her in the fire garden . . . And though I hear it is a sin, a crime, what I do, and wish and feel for you still—my flower, my fawn—I would never have hurt you, never harm you, *never, never . . .*

"My princess.

"She was my masterpiece once," the fencing master says. "Princess Star."

In tights. Magnificent innocence in your whites. In white with mesh and mask over the face whispering *maitre,* on your knees.

"How vague now you have become, how unrecognizable with your blue vial, your crazy cat—I would never have hurt you."

Drugged into a kind of adulthood. Junked up and falling in slow motion. Saying *never, never,* and you will *never tell anyone ever.*

You are the isolate. With your vial of pure ice. Your pink mouth smeared across the wall. No match for the master.

The fencing master mouthing *masterpiece.*

One scarcely can remember such silence—Unbearable.

And from the house redolent with arches the famous bearded doctor announces: "Either she is speaking the truth and all the fathers are vile, or she is a liar and the patriarchal order is safe."

And she doesn't stand a ghost of a chance.

" . . . a vivid imagination."

" . . . a flawed moral character."

The bomb like a flower opening for forty-three seconds . . . The bomb falling like a kind of never.

Suspended in a kind of bluish liquid.

. . . The target garden on fire.

She did, she did, she tried to hide.

Not a ghost of a chance . . .

Not all the opium in China . . .
Not all the love in the world . . .

Who knows what might have been—had things been different—early on—from the beginning even.

In another world in another time long ago you dreamt. Dreamt of dancing all night. Until your shoes were worn—

Without the surveillance of the fathers.

"This afternoon a curious thing happened to me. The reality of everything began to recede. I felt lonely and inaccessible and forgotten, and had a number of illusions, sometimes vivid and sometimes unreal. There were two sisters, one of whom talked about a river."

The river glistening . . . this is your exquisite.

But oh how now she slips out of last sociabilities—surprisingly effortlessly—surprisingly free of regrets—last impediments. Falling, falling into forgetfulness,

and she wraps herself around the voluptuous—takes it in.

Sucking on the stamen of a poppy smile. Correct me if I'm wrong but that seems to be . . .

She carries her blur and releases it just before he. In the target garden.

. . . that seems to be . . .

The fencing master was arrested and disappeared, as it proved, forever.

You look up. At last you see—at last—someone in the mirror you think you recognize.

You are as light as a feather, as stiff as a board.

"Champion," you say.

"You're a winner."

"The winner's circle . . . "

And then nothing. *Enfin.*

One scarcely remembers such snow—or such silence. The white-lit way. The world low-lit. How soft the edges are. How like smoke the trees have become. Every word you make dissolves now. Look:

The Herbalist's Treasury from the tenth century smile. The poppy, the shield that confers immortality. Brilliant—brilliant— that color. You lift a hand to shield you from the glare and smile.

Moving into her with more force now—*Hey—oh—it's good that way.*

Is that you Ming? The cat smuggled in poor child they looked the other way. School girl rituals and levitations. Devouring butterfly wings. Floating. As light as a feather. Letting go now of the candy box—sweet and numb. As stiff as a board. And the globe.

How slowly and yet how quickly—and with such little effort now—eternity, oblivion . . . At last you subtract your image from the mirror. This is your Exquisite Hour.

And the snow says: *Hey.*

The space now wider and wide until it seems—and she is straddling it—sucking on a string of pearls.

At last you see—at last—someone in the mirror you think you recognize. And I am happier than I have ever felt, she thinks. I am more or less happy in my life . . . as if I belong here.

And so perhaps for the first, for the first time. For the first time she looks into the mirror and she likes what she sees. For the first time.

Licking the last flakes from the pane. The demented waltz step and smiles. A row of girls holding hands out for a stroll—strange—vanishing in the snow.

In the last village

But someone reach me
A fragrant cupful
Of dark light, that
I might rest; it would be sweet
To drowse in the shade.
                    HOLDERLIN

And look, how we've come to this place at last—

This *at last*

The two women standing at that precipice, white bed,
white and floating world—waving. They say to us, *at last.*

It's as if—It's as if we've been waiting a lifetime for you.

The transluscence of their touch. At last.

At the gate of the white village, the quotation is from
Valéry. It says: and they read it in unison, dragging their
fingers slowly over each word,

"Friend, do not come in here without desire."

as we move into the ecstasies of the end together, at last.

Lilting gorgeous world. Aureole.

In the white village the white-haired women waving. In the last
village of Z. All is beauty.

Everything I loved or wanted or feared is here. Following
the gleam.

The room perfumed. Scent of lavender.

You'll be asleep soon.

No more insomnia. Lavender, a lovely sedative. And the
silence.

How muffled the world suddenly—as if walking through snow

to the last village of Zenka, perched on a hill

where forever resides, and hasn't it been nice?

The women comb each other's hair and laugh and talk until
they fall

Sailing, sailing into port. Clutching now a child's
almanac—or so it seems,

remembering

there's the dazzling village of *A,* with its airplanes, sweet apples . . .

they turn to face the day, and beyond,

a picture book, a book of days,

strange . . .

R is for the way the rose clings

The traveler from an era almost completely disappeared now (two trunks, a hat box) picks up her day book and begins to write in a beautiful old hand, a penmanship, "Darling, you can't believe the fruit here,"

"I am listening to Billie Holiday on the Victrola. It always reminds me of you . . . " A voice imprint.

Sailing, sailing into port, faded rooms and cigarettes and postage stamps. A can of talc. A comb and brush set. On the bureau a yearbook from the college called Vassar. It's cocktail time. Sherry or scotch or maybe bourbon?

Lilting amber world.
They smile, draw the letter zed in talc, my love.

Come my dove—(intensifying to rose) come to bed now. (just the thought)

Everything suddenly muffled
She's dreaming on the lip, on the edge of the known world
remembering
Her hand reading across the pillow to outline the lips—the whole
room perfumed . . .

Qu'est-ce que c'est que ça?

And as irresistible as it's all been—

They press the tiny book of delirium into my palm . . . as beautiful as it's all been . . .

it's as if, as if—

now at the edge of the bed: your gorgeousness

And they whisper, giggling, "this must be Paradise . . . "

streamers flying after

and the women waving, holding on just a little—
lingering

and then, *at last*

the way the lip cleaves
the way the lip clings

intensify

Where eternity resides, where rising up from the sea—
eternity

"We dine on trays next to the fire and wait for you."

On that extraordinary precipice

Fourteen years ago—another life really—we stood in downy
green, and it seemed to me—

it seemed—in dreamy green . . .

the room drained (but gently) now of color.

The voices have known or read of this love story. Some of them re-
member it better than others. But none of them remembers it com-
pletely. And none of them has completely forgotten . . .

And she reads aloud from *The Fourth Book of Desire* which is
sometimes called the *Third* depending on your numbering sys-
tem. Though numbers scarcely matter now—or matter now too
much perhaps.

walking through fog and lavender

They pat my head. They take my ink-stained hands.

"You love the luminous gray days still—just as when you were a
child. Little and much has changed since then"

They hand me goodbye and an early rose—without thorns. In the white room, where

"We sit next to the fire . . . "

flushed

(Intensify to rose then one more time). We sit next to the fire, rosy

cup of radiant, cup of mysterious universe
they sip lemon balm
and inquire after the 26 figures

cup of desire

Leafing through the dreamy alphabet. *It's as if*—Back in the dazzling village of *A*. In morning. The A.M.—home. Village of percussive Aishah. Distant Ana-Julia. Inaccessible Alice. Sweet apple. Out of reach. Aureole. There's a circle of light around the world.

The illuminated alphabet.

All that longing in the letter *C.*

In the moment I realize I will have to say goodbye. Someday soon have to say goodbye.

Day after day of pleasure in the village of cats. Lapping. Purr. Carrying night and stars in our fur.

muffled

One scarcely remembers such white

And they walk the blurry edge now. They help each other into
the white bed. Turning, turning down a linen sheet, a page

recalling how their darling Laura, long ago, in the village
of *L* scattered rose petals for her lover.

They hold votives now for all the lovers—"Oh it doesn't
seem possible—"

and press lavender under my last lip

and delirium

"Oh it doesn't seem possible that—"

waving and waving

As we delay a little, stay, as we prolong, elongate . . .

"You have been missed with a capital *M,* tell us—

"Are you still carrying around that large black artist's
book and writing everything down?"

Yes.

And there's Helen. With her dark crown of curls and her banners. She holds my hand in winter.

In the perfect shelter of *H*

Irresistible as it's been . . .

Shining grave emblems on a field of light

And in the blinding village of *I*—

A place that burns brighter than a million suns . . .

Between the god and the light

where Ilene has presided.

Take me to the other side.

Gorgeous lilting world

In the beautiful land of Judith—

The women pressing forever

"just as when you were a child . . . "

"Are you still writing in that large black book?"

And the mother Rose—

and the other mother Lily (how she grieved)—grieves
still . . .

A garden of mothers.

Passing down their passion bouquets—so fragrant, so—

As a child she liked to . . .

at last.

and stuffing flower petals now into our mouths,

in the white village. The two women waving and waving and
squinting yes, this must be Paradise—

reaching for the atlas

or maybe Paris.

There is a moment without music. In memory of Marguerite Duras.

"Friend do not come here without desire."

remembering once more the shining river

Streamers flying

. . . like the river clings

like the hip—

Stay

someday soon have to say—

And another river like plums running dark

where they are expected—

reaching for—

reaching

zed

speechlessness

And they press oblivion into my palm, and they press calm

a fragrant cupful of dark light

In the white village. Where our bones, gorgeous alphabet
will glow on the beach.

And they read in unison from *The Book of Desire* one last time

Voluptuous world

Following the gleam of her body down

drinking from her cup

of mysterious paradise

Aureole.

Gorgeous.

Gorgeousness . . .

more—

3 March 1996

Notes

"The Women Wash Lentils"

The Book of Oysters is Eleanor Clark's *The Oysters of Locmariaquer*. *The First Book of Desire* is my own *Ghost Dance*. *The Fourth Book of Desire* is *The American Woman in the Chinese Hat*.

"Her Ink-Stained Hands"

Ghost Dance and *The American Woman in the Chinese Hat* make appearances in this piece as well.

"Make Me Dazzle"

"Exhultation is the Going" is Emily Dickinson.

"Anju Flying Streamers After"

Lines from Marguerite Duras's screenplay *India Song* appear in this piece. As do quotations from a letter from Bhanu Kapil. Pages 145–147 are an extended excerpt from that letter.

"The Devotions"

Italicized lines are from *India Song*.

"Sappho Sings the World Ecstatic"

Italicized text is Sappho. Quotations are from Gertrude Stein. Lines in dark type are from the shot lists of Maya Deren's films *At Land* and *Meshes of the Afternoon*.

"Exquisite Hour"

Part of the inspiration here is from the life of the writer Anna Kavan. Also making an appearance is "The Twelve Dancing Princesses" by Jacob and Wilhelm Grimm. You will recognize by now the lilting lines of *India Song*.

The Oysters of Locmariaquer, by Eleanor Clark; The University of Chicago Press, 1964.

The Legend of Maya Deren, A Documentary Biography and Collected Works, Volume I, Part II by Clark, Hodson and Neiman; Anthology Film Archives, 1988.

India Song by Marguerite Duras; Grove Press, 1976.

Grimm's Fairy Tales, Nine Stories by Jacob and Wilhelm Grimm; Penguin, 1995.

The Case of Anna Kavan, A Biography by David Callard; Peter Owen, London, 1993.

About the Author

Carole Maso is the author of *The American Woman in the Chinese Hat*, *AVA*, *The Art Lover*, and *Ghost Dance*. She teaches at Brown University.